I0554342

EPSILON CITY

A STONEWALL CHRONICLES
NOVEL

HERBERT GROSSHANS

EPSILON CITY
Copyright © 2024 by Herbert Grosshans

ISBN: 979-8-88653-243-2

Melange Books, LLC
White Bear Lake, MN 55110
www.melange-books.com

Published in the United States of America.

Cover Design by Ashley Redbird Designs

THE STONEWALL CHRONICLES NOVELS

Outpost Epsilon (the prequel)

1 - A New Dawn

2 - Epsilon City

3 - Mysteries of Epsilon

[1]

"Epsilon City is different from any city on other planets populated by Humans because Humans did not build it. Giant ants built the dome centuries ago. They abandoned it after parasites invaded the hive and killed off the majority of the ant population. It stood empty for over a century until some enterprising settlers decided the honeycombed structure would make a safe place for Humans to live in. The ants, they call their race *Uur*, are ingenious engineers and builders. The air inside the dome is cool and dry compared to the outside air and stays at a constant twenty-three degrees Celsius."

Houston took a sip from the bottle in his hand. Looking across his audience in the bus he smiled. "Of course, some of our guests, usually of non-human species, of which we don't get too many, find it too cold and we had to install heaters in their apartments."

"What happened to the parasites?" a young woman asked from the rear of the transporter.

"They eventually moved out and died of starvation after their hosts left."

The woman shook her red hair and gave a sigh of relief. "I'm sure

1

glad to hear that. Wouldn't want any creepy-crawlies all over my body."

Houston studied her more closely. His eyes lingered for a moment on her generous display of breasts. *Wouldn't mind roaming my hands all over your body.* Smiling, he said, "As far as I know there would have been no danger of that. Apparently, the parasites were as large as housecats on Earth. Rest assured, when Humans arrived on Epsilon, the dome was empty of life."

"Why didn't the original owners move back?" another passenger asked.

"They built another dome about fifty miles west of here. The area around their new hive is mostly desert and rocks, which gives them more control of who moves in with them."

"How do you know that? Or are you just making this up?" The redheaded woman seemed to challenge him.

Houston frowned, but then he laughed. "We do communicate with the indigenous people. Others have asked that question before, you know."

"Thank you. I guess you should know what you're talking about, after all...you live here." She hesitated slightly before asking, "Are you living in the dome?"

"Yes, I am."

"How large is the dome?"

Houston turned his attention toward the man who asked. Then he looked out of the transporter's window. They were still far enough away to see the top of the huge cone. "It rises about one thousand two-hundred feet into the sky," he said, almost proudly. "From its apex one can see the first hive of the Uur nation to the west. The giant mushrooms of the jungle seem almost small when viewed from the top of Epsilon City. It is a marvelous view."

"How many people live in the city now?"

"According to the latest count nearly ten thousand call Epsilon City their home."

"That's a lot of people."

Houston chuckled. "Believe it or not, there is room for twenty thousand more."

"How do you keep the dinosaurs from entering the area around the city?" another man asked.

"The whole compound is surrounded by a tall electric fence. It keeps out anything trying to invade us." He smiled. "Except for the ones roaming the sky. The larger ones we shoot down with missiles, the smaller ones with flash rifles."

The transporter neared the huge structure and headed for a gaping hole at the base. As the transporter drove through the opening, a large tunnel appeared ahead, winding its way into the dome's interior.

"This tunnel leads all the way up to the top," Houston explained.

Artificial mini-suns lit up the smooth road surface and the walls. In their light, smaller tunnels could be seen leading away from the main road.

"First-time visitors may find everything a bit confusing, but in reality, this whole city is well planned. The tunnels leading away on every level split into an apparent maze, but after exploring them, one finds order in the layout. As I said before, the dome is a marvel of engineering. Our own engineers have taken great care not to interfere with the basic design."

The transporter entered one of the side tunnels and came to a halt in a large cavern-like room. Bright light flooded in from a huge opening in one wall. The giant umbrellas of the nearby mushroom jungle could be seen in the distance, which meant this room was still in the lower half of the dome.

"Ladies and gentlemen, we have arrived. I hope you all have a pleasant stay." Houston smiled and made a little bow when a few people applauded. Then he turned and stepped off the transporter.

He walked toward the opening and stood close to the edge. Looking out, he could see the bubble that housed the offices of the Trading Commission. Far to the right rested the spaceship that brought the latest wave of newcomers to Epsilon. Near the Trading Commission's habitat stood two large ships...freighters who delivered supplies from Earth and would take back goods destined for trade with other planets. The group in his transporter was composed mainly of merchants and scientists, who wouldn't stay long. From his vantage point he could see other transporters being loaded with the ones who planned to stay; some for a limited time, maybe a few years, some forever. Fortune hunters, gamblers, prospectors, and farmers with their families. Possibly even one or two con men. A few of them might realize their dream, most would be disappointed, finding nothing but misery, some even death.

Thinking about his own ambitions and disappointments, he stared at the distant clouds hovering above the brown blanket of mushroom umbrellas. A lone *Dactyl* glided into view from the east but was lost again in the mist rising from *Death Valley*, a giant swamp bordering the *Purple Sea.*

"Excuse me..."

He turned around at the sound of the voice. His eyebrows lifted slightly when he recognized the redheaded woman who had been so inquisitive. "Yes?"

She gave him a shy smile. "I don't mean to bother you, but I think I need your help."

"You think?" He returned her smile. "I'm not sure if I can or want to help you. It depends what it is you want from me," he said cautiously.

She shouldered her duffle bag. Then she shrugged and put it on the floor. "Damn thing is getting heavy," she said, smiling uncertainly.

"Well?" Houston stared at her, getting impatient. He studied her casually but with some interest. Attractive women like her didn't usually come to Epsilon, at least not alone. And none of them would approach him and ask for help.

The woman held out a hand. "My name is Tara Turner. This is my first time on Epsilon."

He shook her hand, chuckled. "I would have never guessed, Miss Turner."

She didn't smile, only lifted the corners of her lips. "I..." Her shoulders slumped a little. "Never mind, I'll find help somewhere else." She took her duffle bag and turned to walk away.

On an impulse, he grabbed her arm. "I never said I wouldn't help you."

She looked at him over her shoulder. "No, but you didn't offer it either."

Looking into her green eyes, he felt compelled to ask, "Where are you staying?"

She shrugged. "I was told there are shelters for people like me. I can't afford the exuberant prices of the luxury hotels."

"You can stay at my place." He said it only to be polite, not really expecting her to accept.

To his surprise, she said, "I will if your offer is sincere."

He had committed himself. There was no turning back. "It is," he said.

"I don't even know your name."

"David Houston. Dave to my friends."

"I guess I'll have to call you David?"

"Nobody does." He chuckled. "Call me Dave. The only person who ever called me David is dead."

"Who?"

"My mother." He threw one last look out of the huge window. The clouds seemed darker and closer. It looked like a storm was moving in. "Come on. My scooter is one level up."

She followed him in silence as he walked back to the main road. The rest oft the passengers had already disappeared. Houston walked briskly. The woman seemed to be struggling with her duffle bag as she tried to keep up with him climbing the incline of the road.

"Is it far?" she called.

He stopped and waited for her to catch up. "I guess you're not a mountain climber," he said.

"I've climbed mountains. It is part of my job," she said when she reached him.

"What do you do?"

"I'm a geologist."

"Give me your bag. I'll carry it," he offered.

She seemed hesitant, but then she shrugged and gave it to him. "I'm willing to follow you to your place, even though I don't know you. Might as well trust you with my stuff."

He threw the duffle bag across his broad shoulders. "I've never robbed anyone," he growled. "I'm not going to start now." He turned and trudged on.

"Thank you," she said. "Just so you know...I don't have much money."

"I haven't asked for any."

"No, you haven't." She paused, struggling with her next words. "I...I could pay you in other ways...if that's okay."

"I've never asked a woman to pay me that way, either." He glanced at her. "But with you I might make an exception."

She stumbled and almost fell. He reached out to steady her. When he looked into her face, he thought he saw a small tear in one corner of her eye. "I'm sorry," he said soothingly. "It was a joke. You have nothing to fear from me. I would never ask you to do anything you are not willing to give freely. And this would not be given freely. I don't rape women."

She smiled bravely, swallowing. "Thank you. I guess I'm not such a bad judge of character after all."

"This time. Next time you may not be so lucky. Epsilon is a frontier world. You're quite safe in this city. On the rest of the planet..." He shook his head. "Totally different story. Take my advice. Don't trust anyone. A woman with your looks shouldn't be traveling alone."

"You're not the first person to tell me that," she said, sighing. "All of my friends warned me against this trip."

"You said you're a geologist. Shouldn't you be with a group? I mean, scientists usually travel together as a team."

"I'm not here professionally."

"Why are you here?"

"To find my brother."

"Your brother? He is on Epsilon?"

She nodded. "He came here five years ago. He's a geologist, like me. Wanted to make his fortune."

Houston laughed dryly. "Don't we all?"

"What do you mean?"

He turned into another tunnel. "We're almost there."

"What did you mean with your last remark?" She insisted on hearing his answer.

6

"I spent two years in that insect-infected jungle dodging lizards and chasing my dream, digging for gemstones. Sure, I found plenty, but they're worthless here and you're not allowed to take them off planet. Nobody tells you that until you find some and try to cash them in." He chuckled humorlessly. "They let you trade them in for equipment so you can keep on digging."

"I don't understand. Who are *they*?"

"The Solar Union. Everything here is controlled by the Union. The Trading Commission will take the gems off your hands for a pittance. Welcome to *Hell*, pretty innocent lady. With all the riches buried in the ground of this forsaken ball, nobody is able to earn enough money to ever leave again. The Solar Union sees to that."

She gave him an inquiring look. "Is that what happened to you?"

Without answering her question, he stopped in front of a small scooter. "Hop on. I'm living on the fifty-sixth floor. We are on floor twenty-three." He mounted the two-seater, waited until she climbed behind him. "Put your arms around my chest," he instructed. "I don't want you falling off."

The scooter floated on a thin cushion of air. It began moving without making a sound. Houston switched on the low-level siren to alert others of his approach as they moved on the wide road. The tunnel spiraled with a steady incline toward the apex of the cone-city.

When they reached floor fifty-six, Houston slowed the speed of his scooter and took a side tunnel. Stopping in front of a door, he said, "This is my humble place." He parked the scooter beside the door and, pressing his hand on a plate in its center and entering his password into the tiny keyboard, he waited until the door swung open.

"Enter the lair of the Spider," he said, smiling.

She hesitated for a moment.

When he saw the sudden fear in her eyes, he chuckled. "Forgive my sense of humor. I'm probably as apprehensive as you. This is the first time I've invited a woman into my apartment."

"I guess I should feel honored," she said, rewarding him with a smile. "As long as you don't think of me as a fly." She followed him into the room and looked around. "It's nice," she said.

He laughed. "It may not be fancy, but, as the saying goes, it is home. A tiny kitchen, a small living room, and a smaller bedroom. Oh, the bath-cubicle is over there. It has a toilet and a sink. No shower or tub. We have to use the community washrooms for that. They allow us only so much water. You can go right in if you want to freshen up."

"I would. Thank you." She reached for her duffle bag. "I won't use up all your water. I promise." Smiling, she headed for the indicated door.

He watched her disappear into the bath-cubicle. Then he went to the small fridge and took out a can of beer. A luxury he allowed himself only once a week, usually on weekends, but somehow, he figured he needed it.

———

Tara Turner ran her fingers through her hair and shook a few carrot-red strands out of her face. "I don't know how to thank you for your kindness," she said.

Houston smiled and dismissed her concern with a wave of his hand. "You'll get the opportunity sooner or later, don't worry about it. I couldn't let a helpless girl loose on a strange planet and wonder for the rest of my life what kind of trouble she might have fallen into."

She pulled her lips into a mock pout and her eyes flashed green. "I'm not exactly a helpless little girl. I'm twenty-five years old."

He laughed, studying her without being too obvious. He had to admit, she was a beauty. She changed her traveling clothes for a pair of shorts and a blouse that molded itself around her breasts. It was evident she didn't wear any support under the thin material. Not that they needed support.

She noticed his scrutinizing looks and blushed lightly. He looked away. "How long are you planning to stay?" he asked, trying to hide his embarrassment.

She shrugged. "Until I find my brother or..." she hesitated, "or until I find out what happened to him."

"That could take some time."

"I know, but don't worry, I'm not going to stay long in Epsilon City if he isn't here. I might have to go searching for him."

"In the jungle? All by yourself?" He eyed her, his expression skeptical. "Epsilon is a large planet. The jungle seems endless, and the deserts stretch forever. Your brother might be anywhere, and there is danger everywhere. This is not a place for a young woman. Especially one who is alone."

She gave him a calculating look. "Would you be willing to help me looking for him?"

"I don't think so. I have no problem giving you a place to stay and trying to keep you out of trouble, but going into that lizard-infected jungle?" He shook his head vehemently. "I have no such desires. Not anymore."

Her green eyes looked thoughtful. "Are you happy here, Dave?"

"Am I happy here?" He chuckled grimly. "What kind of question is that? Of course I'm not happy here. I'd give anything to get off this stinking planet."

"Maybe I can help you."

"You?" He couldn't help but laugh. "It seems to me you need my help more than I need yours."

"I was under the impression you hated the Union."

"I never said that." He wondered where she was heading. Maybe she was a Union-spy trying to trip him up. He didn't trust anyone, not in Epsilon City...or anywhere else on this planet.

"Not in so many words." She tilted her head. "Didn't you tell me the Union controls the gem trade?"

"Yes, I did, because it is true." No harm in admitting that. "Actually, it isn't the Union, it's the Trading Commission."

"Isn't that the same thing?"

"Some people seem to think so." He didn't say any more.

She bent forward and looked into his eyes. "I am going to trust you, Dave. With my life, my future. I need a friend badly and you seem like a nice and descent guy. Yes, I need you, but I know you need me too, because I can help you get off this planet."

"If you can somehow miraculously conjure up ten-thousand credits and put them into my hand, I would believe you. But you can't, so please stop playing with my mind." He was annoyed at her for even suggesting she could help him get off Epsilon when it was clear she couldn't.

"You are right, I don't have that kind of money, but I know some people who have."

"Who?"

"The Belter's Consortium."

"What?" He threw back his head and laughed.

She waited until he finished laughing before she said, "It is not a joke. I am deadly serious."

"Why would the Belters help me? I'm an Earthman, a surface crawler. Most Belters hate us because we are able to walk in the sun, walk under trees, swim in big lakes, or the ocean, breathe natural air, while they hide inside hollowed out asteroids and have to breathe artificially created air. They never see the sun except on viewing screens, never smell the fresh, crisp air in spring or run naked in the rain." He laughed again. "I don't know any Belters and I have no reason to expect help from them."

"I'm a Belter," she said softly.

"You don't look like one."

"How should I look?" she asked, an impish smile playing around her lips. "I know you've been scrutinizing me."

"Only because you're so beautiful."

"I shouldn't be beautiful to be a Belter?"

"You should be taller and thinner."

"I guess you don't know much about the Belt and the people who live in it. I am five foot two and I weigh fifty-three kilograms. I was born on Dawson, an asteroid almost two hundred miles in diameter. The surface is dotted with huge habitats where we grow trees, shrubs, flowers, and grass. We even have small lakes. We can do most of the things Earth people can do. As for my height, well, all of the habitats have artificial gravity generators to create one g. Does that answer your question?"

"I guess it does. And more."

"There are tall people on Earth. Some of them are taller than people born on an asteroid." Her smile seemed to mock him. "You're not one of the tall people, though. What happened?"

"Nothing happened. There are plenty of people my height on Earth. I'm happy with my five eight."

"Good for you. Another thing, contrary to what most of you Earthers believe, Belters don't hate you and we don't envy you, either. Earth is overcrowded, depleted of most of its resources. The water is polluted, as is the air, and the weather is unpredictable. Believe me when I tell you we are happy where we are. I'd almost say the opposite is true...Earthers hate us." Her words were proud, and her eyes flashed angrily.

He found her incredibly attractive. "You've made your point, but you still haven't answered my question. Why would the Belter's Consortium want to help me?"

"In exchange for *your* help."

"*My* help?" he repeated, giving her a thoughtful look. "Who are you, actually, Miss Tara Turner? If that is your real name."

"It is my name, and what I told you is true." She spoke rapidly, sounding urgent. "I am here to find my brother. At least that is part of my mission. You see, he was sent here five years ago to report on the conditions of this planet, to find out if rumors are true that the Solar Union is preventing gems and drugs to be traded freely. Many Belters who live on asteroids with no or very little gravity suffer from many deficiencies, for instance loss of bone density. Most old Belters have osteoporosis. We need some of the drugs found on Epsilon. We need to have free access to them."

When she stopped to take a deep breath, he interrupted her, "Are you telling me you're a spy?"

She nodded. "You could say that."

"Who are you working for?"

"The PIA."

"Never heard of them?"

"It is short for Planetary Intelligence Agency, the secret service of the Belter's Consortium." Her facial expression was anxious, and her eyes studied his reaction.

He sat silent for a long time, staring at the forgotten drink in his hand. "You don't look and act like a spy," he finally said.

She chuckled. "Isn't that the idea? Did you expect a sign around my neck saying *I am a spy*?"

"Of course not. What I mean is you don't come across like a tough, hardboiled, cold-eyed crime fighter. You know...the characters they show in the entertainment holograms."

"You don't really believe those characters actually exist, do you?" Her laugh seemed strained. "Even if they did, I'm not that kind of a spy. When I said I was a geologist I spoke the truth. The Agency hired me to search for my brother and possibly find out more about Epsilon. Of all the colonists and fortune hunters coming here, none have returned. Sure, casual visitors and dignitaries come back after getting the supervised tour, but people who came to stay for a while haven't. People are beginning to wonder what happened to them."

"I can tell you. The same thing that happened to me. They are stuck here. Every day here is a fight for survival. If the jungle or the native wildlife doesn't swallow you up, the laws of the Solar Union and the restrictions put upon every citizen and immigrant make certain you stay buried here." His words sounded bitter in his own ears. Was it possible that this young woman could actually help him to finally leave this hell behind? He hardly dared hope.

She put a hand on his. The touch of her soft, warm hand sent tiny shivers through his body. "Help me and you don't need to stay buried any longer. This could be your chance to escape. You don't have to go back to Earth. There are plenty of asteroid communities who would welcome you with open arms. They need fresh blood. Life in the Belt is not bad."

He shook his head. "I don't know. I can't organize an expedition and search party into the jungle. It takes money to pay for equipment, guards, weapons..."

"How do the new colonists get to their designated areas?"

"The Trading Commission provides them with a transporter, but only to their destination. After that they are on their own. They are stuck wherever they are sent until they can bring back things of value to trade in for equipment. Many of them die within the first few months unless they can join up with an established community."

"People live in those communities. How do they get around in the jungle?"

"On armored vehicles and local pack animals, which they have to catch and domesticate, or just plain old walking on their own two legs.

Life in those frontier towns is hard, be it a farming community or a place where fortune hunters and prospectors dwell." Acutely aware of her touch, he pulled his hand away, feeling uneasy by her sudden intimate gesture.

She seemed to notice his discomfort and smiled, rosy color creeping into her cheeks. "Sorry," she said, "Don't read me wrong. I'm not trying to seduce you or anything like that to entice you to help me."

You being here is seduction enough. He grinned lopsidedly. "Having a woman touch me makes me uncomfortable."

"You don't like women?"

That made him chuckle. "Of course I like women. It's just...I haven't been close to anyone for a long time. Living here isolates you from others, especially when all you think of is survival. Believe me, I would like nothing more than take you into my arms and kiss you, hold you tight and..." He didn't finish the sentence, suddenly embarrassed.

Her eyes were large when she looked at him. "I might just let you do that."

Her words shocked him a little. "You surprise me," he said slowly. "Yesterday when I made a joke after you offered to pay me with...you know..."

"With sex?"

"Well...yes, with sex, you acted afraid as if I might take you up on it. Now you tell me..." He shook his head. "You don't mean it. Maybe you are trying to seduce me after all, but with an ulterior motive."

"Isn't that what women do? Seduce a man they like?"

"Under different circumstances I would believe you are sincere, but I know right now you are desperate and willing to do almost anything to get someone to help you. As I told you yesterday, I don't rape women."

Her smile was warm and her eyes grateful. She reached out and touched his hand again. "You are a good person," she whispered, her eyes suddenly filling with tears. "You are right, I am desperate. I need someone to help me find my brother."

This time he didn't pull his hand away. "I'll see what I can do," he said softly. "But no promises, okay?"

She nodded bravely. "Okay. Thank you, Dave."

"Don't thank me yet."

She delicately dabbed at her eyes. "Sorry about that. I don't usually cry. You must think I'm a weak little girl. Please, don't pity me. I can take care of myself, but maybe this time I've taken on too much." She took a small handkerchief from her pocket and wiped her nose. "You mentioned frontier towns. How do the prospectors travel between Epsilon City and their towns?"

"The Trading Commission has an armored bus traveling back and forth from Epsilon City to Lizard's Tongue. They might give you permission to use it if you have a legitimate reason...one that suits their purpose. Of course, there are other ways. Apparently, there are a couple of airplanes being operated out of Star City, but traveling in the air is dangerous. Too many flying predators prowling the airways. They might decide to attack the plane, mistaking it for a rival. Some travelers use armored land vehicles to brave the jungle. It is a treacherous journey. You never know when a carnosaur is hungry enough to challenge your presence. The only way to be relatively safe is in a huge armored and armed bus."

"How about using a scooter?"

"Only a fool or someone with a death wish would use a scooter to travel through the thick jungle and swamp. Especially not for a long trek like you're proposing."

"How far is it anyway to the next frontier town?"

He lifted his shoulder. "Star City is about three hundred miles north of here, but it is not considered a frontier town anymore. It has grown these last five years. The next one is Emerald Lake, three hundred miles northeast of Star City. There are large farming communities within five hundred miles north of Star City. I have no idea how many frontier towns and camps actually exist. They are spread over a large area to the north."

"What's to the south?"

"Desert. Endless hot and dry desert. No sane man would go into that." Houston looked up when someone pounded against the door to his apartment. "I wonder who that is."

He got up and opened the door.

Two men dressed in the uniform of Security confronted him. "Are you David Houston?"

"Yes, I am. What can I do for you?"

"You have a woman by the name of Tara Turner with you?"

"Yes, she's with me. What about her?"

One of the security men pushed Houston aside and forced his way past him into the apartment.

Tara had left her seat at the table and faced the men by the door.

"Miss Tara Turner? Epsilon City Security. Please, come with us." He spoke with a harsh, authoritative voice that left no room for arguments.

———

Houston sat in the back of the Security vehicle. He sensed Tara's uneasiness and reached over to touch her arm. "Things will be all right," he said, soothingly.

She shook her head. "I'm scared," she whispered. Then she said aloud, addressing the Security men in the front seat, "Why won't you tell me what this is all about?"

"You will be told," one of them said with a harsh voice.

"I did nothing wrong," she insisted. "I'm a visitor here and I demand the respect I deserve." She looked at Houston when none of the men responded. "Can't you do something?"

He shrugged. "There is nothing to do but wait until we get to the Security office. I'm sure this is just a misunderstanding."

The vehicle glided silently down the corridor. No one traveling from the opposite direction could miss the bright flashing lights in the front and back of the vehicle. They finally took a side tunnel on the second floor and halted in front of a brightly lit barred window. Beside it, a steel door led into the room that was visible through the window. Above the door a sign proclaimed this as *Epsilon City Security Headquarters.*

The guard in the passenger seat got out of the vehicle and opened the rear door. "Please, go through that door," he instructed Tara. He looked at Houston. "You can accompany the lady if you so wish."

Houston smiled grimly. "Don't worry, I will." He got out on the other side and walked around the vehicle. Tara waited until he stood beside her and let him open the door for her.

A guard stood on the other side of the door, a flash rifle in his hand. He pointed at the counter across the room. "Please, register at the desk."

Houston walked beside the woman, who held on to his sleeve. She seemed scared and helpless.

She certainly doesn't act like a spy. Unless she's such a good actress.

The uniformed Security man behind the desk looked up as Houston and Tara approached. His eyes fixed on Tara. "Are you Miss Turner?" he asked.

She nodded. "Yes, I am."

"One moment." The man ran his hand across his computer screen in front of him and nodded. "You've been expected," he said. "Have a seat." He looked at Houston. "You too, Mr. Houston!"

"I wasn't told to come here. I came because I wanted to. How am I suddenly involved?"

The man glared at him. "You involved yourself, Mr. Houston. Now, have a seat and wait!"

Houston looked around and found a bench at the end of the room. "Come on," he said to Tara. "Don't worry, we'll straighten this out. Somebody screwed up somewhere."

They waited possibly ten minutes, when a door beside the front desk opened and another uniformed man came out. "Please, accompany me," he told them.

Houston noticed that the man was armed, but his weapon was holstered. That was a good sign. There was a good chance they would not be shot the moment they walked through the door. At least, that's what he hoped. He didn't trust Security men or soldiers. You never knew when they wanted to try out their weapons on an unsuspecting victim.

The man walked ahead of them. Also a good sign.

He smiled at Tara. "I think everything is going to turn out okay," he said softly.

She smiled bravely. "I trust you," she whispered. Grabbing his hand, she squeezed it tightly. He noted her sweaty palm.

This girl isn't acting, he thought. She really is scared.

The Security man took them through a couple of rooms filled with desks occupied by men and women. None of them paid them any attention as they walked past them. They ended up in a small room with only one desk in it and a couple of chairs.

Behind the desk sat a fat, bald man. One look into his face told Houston he was going to be trouble.

"They are all yours," the Security man said, turned and left. The door closed behind him with an audible click.

The fat man studied them silently. Houston couldn't tell the color of his eyes. They were hidden behind fatty tissues that looked like tiny sausages on either side of his surprisingly thin, hooked nose. His nose surely looked out of place above his thick lips. Enormous bushy eyebrows made him look fierce, like an angry Swamp Dragon about to attack. He had no chin and no neck. His jowls hung across rolls of fat that sat on his bulky shoulders where his neck should have been.

"Tara Turner and David Houston," he said at last. It wasn't a question but a statement. His voice sounded like the grating of a pair of hinges screaming to be oiled.

Houston sank into one of the chairs without asking for permission. He was beginning to get annoyed and angry. "Why are we here?" he asked.

"I will be asking the questions," the fat man told him.

"All right. Go ahead. What do you want to know," Houston said belligerently.

"What is your relationship with Miss Turner?"

"My relationship?"

The man's hidden eyes bored into Houston's. "Yes, your relationship?"

"There is no relationship."

"And yet you offered her a place to stay in your unit. Why?"

"Because she had no other place to go. Besides, what makes you think I asked her to stay in my unit?"

The chair the fat man sat in creaked when he moved his bulk. Bending across the desk, he said, "Don't deny anything. Our security cameras recorded your encounter from the moment she stepped off the transporter until you and Miss Turner entered your unit."

"I see. I guess I forgot that every move we honest citizens are making is recorded by Security. It seems you have your spy-cameras hidden in every corner of Epsilon City."

"A necessary precaution to keep law and order." His bushy eyebrows drew together into one straight hairy bar. "Why did Miss Turner come to you, Mr. Houston?"

"Why did she come to me?"

"That's what I asked. Am I speaking in an alien language?"

"You might as well, because I don't understand the question."

Their interrogator heaved a big sigh. It sounded like the hissing of a Firespitter. "Let me rephrase it then...why did Miss Turner turn to you for help?"

"I told you that already. She had no other place to stay."

"You did tell me that didn't you?" He looked at Tara. "There are hostels in Epsilon City, Miss Turner. What is the purpose of your visit?"

"I'm a geologist. I came to Epsilon looking for rare gems. Is that a crime?" She spoke haughtily, almost defiant.

The man actually smiled. "It is not a crime, unless you plan to smuggle them off Epsilon."

"Why would I want to do that?"

"You'd be surprised what people do around here. Why did you not report to Immigration as soon as you arrived, Miss Turner?"

"Immigration? I'm not planning to emigrate to Epsilon. I have no wish to stay here for a long time." She let out a forced little laugh. "If I had any inkling of the welcome I'd be receiving I may not have come here at all."

The interrogator didn't seem to find any humor in her remark. "Most visitors don't plan to stay here but many do. Are you any relation to Gilbert Turner?"

The sudden question seemed to take Tara by surprise. She gasped and said, "You know of him?"

"I know of everyone who comes to Epsilon, Miss Turner, but you didn't answer my question."

"He is my brother."

"Your brother? Hmm." He leaned back into his chair. Houston almost hoped it would break apart under the man's weight. He would have liked to see the fat man sprawl onto the floor.

"Yes, my brother. Do you know where he is?"

"No. He left for one of the mining towns. That was five years ago. We haven't heard from him since. He either changed his name or he is dead," the man said bluntly. "Epsilon is an unforgiving place. There is no room for mistakes once you enter its domain. Either you adapt or you perish. Not everyone is cut out to live here. Not outside." He eyed her with suspicion. "It seems you didn't tell me quite the whole truth about your reason for coming to Epsilon. What else did you keep from me?"

She shook her head with a defiant gesture. "I didn't lie when I said I was a geologist and that I came here looking for gems. That is my profession. I only left out the part that I'm also looking for my brother. Are you going to punish me for that?"

"You are not here to be punished for anything. We are merely trying to establish a valid reason for letting you leave Epsilon City, should you decide to do so. You were supposed to register with Immigration after your arrival and you didn't. That raised a red flag. Why didn't you report?"

"I came in a spaceship. When I boarded the ship, I registered my name and my reason for coming here. Before we landed on Epsilon, I filed all the necessary information with the ship's destination log. I wasn't informed I had to report again after landing. I didn't drop from the sky, you know." Her voice had risen slightly as she spoke, clearly signaling her annoyance.

Seems she's got some fire after all. I find that extremely attractive. Houston glanced at her sideways. *I hope she knows how to control that fire.*

The fat man wasn't impressed by her show of bravado. "You wouldn't be the first person who comes to Epsilon City without proper clearance making up some story how they got lost in space, how they finally found this planet but didn't know its name, and how their private spaceship crash-landed in the jungle." Tiny points of reflected light appeared between the thick folds around his eyes as he regarded Tara. "May I see your ID card, please?"

She lifted the bottom of her blouse a little, revealing a thin traveling belt strapped around her narrow waist. She pulled out a plastic card and handed it to the fat man. He took it without a word and pushed it into a scanner on his desk. Studying the computer screen in the desk's surface, he nodded. "It seems you are indeed who you say you are." He pulled the card out and gave it back. "I hope you have a nice stay, Miss Turner."

She put her card away and rose from her chair. "Is that it?"

He nodded. "You are free to go. Sorry for the inconvenience. Oh, one more word of advice...before you decide to go looking for gems you need to get a permit from the Trading Commission's office." He looked at Houston. "Next time, be more careful whom you choose as your bed companion, Mr. Houston. She might have turned out to be a spy, possibly even murdered you while you slept."

"There is nothing going on between Miss Turner and me. She is not my bed companion, sir," Houston said, annoyed by the man's assumption.

The fat man chuckled, suddenly jovial. "Not yet, but she will be. You'd be a fool to turn away a beautiful woman like that."

Houston grunted and opened the door. A Security man stood

outside, guarding it. "Can you direct us to the exit?" Houston asked him.

The guard nodded and said, "Follow me."

When they stepped into the corridor, Houston said to the guard, "We were brought here in a Security vehicle. How are we going to get home?"

The guard shrugged. "It seems that is your problem." He closed the door and left Houston and Tara standing in the corridor.

[2]

"This is ridiculous!" Houston cursed. "Now what?"

"Is there no public transportation we could use?" Tara asked.

"No, there isn't."

"I guess walking is out of the question?" Tara ventured.

Houston chuckled grimly. "We're talking about seven miles of walking...uphill. That's a long climb."

"What is the alternative?"

"Hitching a ride, but the chance of someone picking up both of us is zero. Everyone drives a scooter like mine. A two-seater. The only vehicles with room for more are official vehicles."

"Then we'll flag down two scooters."

He grinned. "I don't believe you have a problem getting someone to stop. Nobody would pick me up."

"Well, then we'll walk." She grabbed his arm. "Let's go. Walking is healthy. Seven miles isn't that long."

Houston smiled at her enthusiasm and let her drag him along. "We should be grateful it's cool in here. We wouldn't last long if it were as hot and humid as it is outside."

"These tunnels remind me very much of the asteroids," Tara said. "Many Belters live out their life in tunnels. Even though I grew up on the surface of Dawson, under a protective dome, I did spend a fair amount under the surface. These tunnels don't scare me. How about you?"

"Are you asking me if I'm scared?"

She laughed. "Not scared like in...in afraid. I mean...coming from Earth you must have had a hard time getting used to living this way. Inside a tunnel, not seeing the sky when you leave your apartment. This is like living underground."

He remembered roaming the dark alleys between the skyscrapers of Old Chicago, searching the garbage bins behind restaurants for scraps of food while fighting off mutated rats the size of dogs looking for the same thing. He shrugged. "You get used to anything."

"I guess you're right. It was difficult for me the first time I set foot on a planet, seeing the open sky, clouds, feeling rain on my skin, wind in my face. I know what you mean."

The road surface under their feet was smooth, easy to walk on. At first, the gradual incline hadn't seemed so bad, but he was beginning to feel a slight pulling in his leg muscles. He knew it would get worse the longer they walked.

"I wish I had a drink," Tara said. She stuck out her thumb again as another scooter whipped past them. "Doesn't anyone care in this place?" she asked.

"Obviously not." Houston stopped walking and turned to look back. The combined chatter of beeping noises announced the approach of a large number of scooters.

They came around the bend like a swarm of locusts. The men riding them were dressed gaudily. Shaved heads gleamed dully in the light of the artificial suns and the rings in their ears blinked in a multitude of colors.

Tunnel Rats. Young men, who roamed the tunnels on their scooters, finding pleasure in harassing ordinary citizens. Security didn't do anything about them because nobody could prove that they were involved in illegal activities. Houston, however, did not trust them. He had heard stories. None of them encouraging.

They brought their scooters to a halt when they saw Houston and

Tara. Tara didn't seem to be afraid of them. Rather, she appeared delighted when they stopped.

"Hia, beautiful lady," one of them said.

"Out for a stroll with your big brother?" another one asked.

She laughed. "He is not my brother."

"Husband?"

"No, just a friend."

"How would you like to go for a ride?" The speaker pushed out his tongue to show its split tip. His painted eyes studied her openly.

"We're actually going to the fifty-sixth floor," she said brightly. "Can you take us there?"

"I'll take you anywhere you like," the one with the split tongue said. "Hop on."

"No, thank you," Houston said. "We'd rather walk."

Tara gave him an astonished look. "Come on, Dave. These friendly gentlemen are offering us a ride. Isn't that what you wanted?"

"I've changed my mind. Didn't you tell me walking is healthy?"

"I'm tired, Dave," she said, throwing up her hands in exasperation. "I don't think I can go on much longer."

"Yeah, Davy, don't let the beautiful lady walk."

Houston glared at the tattooed youth. "Not even my mother called me *Davy*. Not ever. So don't you call me that!" he snarled.

Their laughter made him even angrier. Long forgotten memories brought back bitter feelings.

Hey, Davy. I fucked your girlfriend last night. She was still a virgin. Poor Davy! Now I spoiled her for you. I made a whore out of her.

He shook his head to banish those memories, but they wouldn't stop.

Davy, your mother is a whore. Just like your girlfriend.

I knew your father, Davy. He's in jail now, Davy. I hear he's everybody's bitch. You want to be my bitch, Davy?

He grabbed the chain with the medallion the youth wore around his neck, twisted. "I suggest you all leave us now!"

Someone touched his arm. He shook the hand away, turned to see it was Tara.

"What's got into you, Dave? They only want to help."

"We don't want their help!" he shouted.

"Why don't you come with us, beautiful lady, and leave your angry friend behind?" the split-tongued youth suggested. "I'll take you to the fifty-sixth floor."

"No!" Houston gave him a shove. The youth lost his balance and fell off his scooter, sprawled on the floor.

His companions laughed. "Davy...Davy..." they chanted. "Angry Davy."

The youth on the ground displayed an ugly face for a split second, but then he joined in the laughter. Rising to his feet, he dusted off his pantaloons. He stood beside his scooter and pointed a finger at Houston. "You should learn to control your anger, Davy. Maybe a lesson is in order."

"A lesson...a lesson..." chanted his friends.

Where the hell is Security when you need them?

A few other scooters had driven by, but none of the drivers seemed to pay any attention to the group blocking part of the road. Houston knew why. Nobody wanted to get involved.

He reached for Tara's hand. "Let's go."

She seemed to get the message, finally, and took his hand, but when Houston tried to move, a couple of the young men blocked his way. The others placed their scooters in a tight ring.

The tall youth he had pushed to the ground opened his mouth in a wide grin. His split tongue flicked across his chin. "You're not really thinking of leaving us, Davy? That would not be polite after we offered you a ride. I want to get to know you and this beautiful lady better."

"If you are planning to harm us, I suggest you'd better forget about it. Security is watching these tunnels, and they should be here any moment," Houston said with false bravado. Even though he wasn't one who backed away from a fight, he knew this was not one he wanted. There were at least fourteen or fifteen youths, most of them taller than him. All of them armed with knifes, which they carried openly strapped to their belts.

He was unarmed. He knew how to fight. Life in the slums of Old

Chicago was not peaceful. You learned to protect yourself at an early age or you didn't survive, but you also learned when it was best to run away.

This was one of those occasions, except there was no place to run.

"Why would you say we want to harm you?" the youth asked. "We only want to have some fun."

"Then seek it elsewhere. I'm not in the mood for fun."

"But we are." The youth leered at Tara. "The beautiful lady and I will be having great fun. I promise."

Houston tried to push him aside, but the others pulled closer. He punched one of them in the face. They responded in kind. Their fists hit hard.

The last thing he saw was Tara's large green eyes staring fearfully at the young men crowding them.

———

Opening his eyes, Houston became aware of a dull pain on the side of his head. When he touched the hurting spot, he winced, pulled his hand away and discovered blood on his fingers.

Groaning, he sat up and surveyed his surroundings. He lay on the side of the road. There was nobody in sight. Staggering to his feet, he heard the soft chiming of an approaching vehicle and clung to the wall to avoid being hit.

A lonely scooter appeared and passed him. The driver probably never saw him hugging the tunnel wall.

He cursed softly when memory began to flood back.

The Tunnel Rats were gone. And so was Tara Turner.

Those bastards! He had heard rumors. Nobody ever talked openly about them. People seemed to be afraid. Afraid of getting involved. If some of those rumors were true, then Houston could understand the fear.

People disappeared. Mostly young women or teenage girls.

"I'll have to find her," he murmured. "It's my fault if anything happens to her. I promised to protect her."

When he heard another vehicle approaching, he stumbled into

the middle of the road. He needed a ride to get home. He'd never make it climbing forty-plus floors. Not in his present condition.

He jumped out of the way when the advancing scooter didn't make any attempts to slow down. The driver was a woman. She swerved as she passed him, missing him by inches. Either she hadn't seen him early enough or she was too afraid to stop and help a stranger.

The lighting was dim were he stood, and he walked on until he came to a part of the tunnel that was brightly lit by the mini-sun embedded in the ceiling. Maybe if the drivers could get a closer look at him, they might be more inclined to offer their help.

Two more scooters passed him without stopping, but the third one slowed down and stopped. A young man. He was bulky, tall and muscular, obviously not afraid of being mugged by a man of Houston's stature.

"You need help?" he asked, his eyes weary as he studied Houston.

"I need a ride to the fifty-sixth floor. That's where I live."

"What happened to you? Did you have an accident?"

"Something like that. I had a run-in with the Tunnel Rats."

"The Tunnel Rats?" The young man's eyes widened. "I...I'm familiar with them. You're lucky to be alive. Hop on. I'll take you home."

Gratefully, Houston climbed behind the driver and held on tightly as they took off. He had a bad headache and his whole body ached where they had punched and kicked him. They must have carried on when he lay unconscious. Every breath he took sent searing pain through his chest.

I'll get you for this! If I have to chase you into the deepest jungle of Epsilon!

The young man dropped him off in front of his apartment. "Take care of that bleeding head of yours," he said, turning his scooter around. "I live on floor forty-three. The name's Nathan Daniels. Everybody knows me there." Then he was off.

Houston waved after him. He had trouble focusing on the keyboard but managed to open his door after a few unsuccessful tries. Sighing, he stumbled into his apartment and fell onto the couch where he lay taking shallow breaths.

I need to wash myself and take some painkillers.

He rose and made it to his bath cubicle. Splashing water into his face and washing off the blood seemed to help. The blood was beginning to crust over the wound on the side of his head. He felt a large bump and flinched when he touched it. Carefully dabbing off the blood, he applied some ointment to keep the wound from becoming infected. Then he swallowed a painkiller and some *Replenisher-dust* and went back into his living room.

The pain subsided within a short time, and he was able to formulate coherent thoughts. He needed to plan his next move. Going to the authorities was not an option. They would do nothing. It was up to him to find Tara. He didn't have much time. However, realizing, there was nothing he could do at the moment, he relaxed and went into the kitchen to make a sandwich.

Even though time was of the essence, he needed to recover from the beating he received. He'd be no good to Tara if his body and reflexes didn't respond when he depended on them.

The Replenisher-dust he took should speed up the healing of his body. He slept for the rest of the day. Before he went to bed for the night, he took more painkillers and Replenisher-dust. When he woke the next morning, he felt he was ready.

Looking in the mirror, he was satisfied. The lump on the side of his face had nearly disappeared. When he touched it, it felt sore, but the pain was bearable, even without painkillers. He knew what he had to do. Searching in a niche in the wall, he removed a small package wrapped inside a towel. After unwrapping it, he stared at the small flash-pistol.

It was illegal to carry weapons inside the dome, but he was desperate. He needed insurance and this was it. The Tunnel Rats carried knives, openly, but there was no guarantee that they didn't possess other weapons.

He took his scooter into the corridor and headed for the forty-third floor.

He was lucky. Nathan Daniels was home. Surprised to see Houston, he opened his door and asked him to come in.

Houston accepted the invitation. When he walked into the room, he became aware of an older woman sitting on the couch. Her eyes scrutinized him with open curiosity.

"Forgive me for barging in on you," Houston said.

"Are you one of my son's friends?" she asked.

Houston smiled. "No, only a stranger he helped in a desperate situation."

She smiled back. "That's my Nathan. He is a good boy. Still picking up stray-animals."

The young man coughed delicately. "She still thinks I'm ten years old. I apologize for her calling you a stray-animal."

"That's not what I meant, Nathan." The woman seemed suddenly flustered and embarrassed. She looked at Houston. "Forgive my blunder."

"Nothing to forgive," Houston said.

"Why are you here?" Nathan asked.

"To ask for your help."

"Help you with what?"

"When I had my altercation with the Tunnel Rats, I wasn't alone. There was a young lady with me."

Nathan's dark face was grave when he said, "She wasn't with you when I picked you up. That means the Tunnel Rats have her. That is bad news. Is she your wife?"

"No. Only someone I promised to protect. I failed her miserably."

"I don't understand how I can help you."

"You seem to know about the Tunnel Rats. Perhaps you know one of their members."

"What makes you think that?"

"The way you reacted when I told you about them." Houston felt suddenly at odds. "I possibly read more into that. Right now, I'm grasping at straws. I should leave."

Nathan stayed silent for a moment. When Houston started to walk toward the door, he said, "No, wait. Don't leave. Maybe I can help you. You are right, I know someone who belongs to the Tunnel Rats. We used to be friends before he joined them."

"Can you introduce me to him?"

Nathan hesitated. "I'd prefer he didn't know how you got his name." He glanced at his mother. "The Tunnel Rats are dangerous. I must protect my mother. I hope you understand."

"I understand. Just tell me his name and where I can find him. Nobody will ever know you where the one who gave me this information," Houston promised.

He left with a name and the place where he could find the man. A bar called *Serpent's Fang*. The man's name was Yan Yamoto.

He spent the remainder of the day in his apartment. When evening came, he was ready. Making certain the small flash-pistol was safely tucked away in the inside pocket of his jacket, he mounted his scooter.

Epsilon City wasn't much different from cities on other planets. There were shops, stores, restaurants and bars. Serpent's Fang was one of them. He knew the clientele who frequented Serpent's Fang. Not a crowd he wanted to mess with.

It was located on the twenty-seventh floor where a cluster of bars and nightclubs had sprung up. Usually, he avoided that part of the city. There were other places on several floors that were quieter and safer.

He parked his scooter in one of the public parking spots on the main road and walked down the wide tunnel with the number twenty-seven in bold letters above the entrance.

A couple of girls stood near the doorway of the bar. They smiled at him and looked him over. "Need company?" one of them asked. Her long dress shimmered and changed colors, became transparent for a split-second, making her appear naked. Then the glimpse of her nude pale body was gone.

"No," he said curtly.

She laughed when she saw his serious face and stepped in front of him. "I can make you forget what bothers you." Her hand reached out and touched his cheek.

He brushed her hand away. "I said no. Are you deaf?"

Her face twisted into an ugly mask. "Am I not good enough for you? You think you'll find someone better in there?"

He forced himself to smile. The last thing he needed right now was a confrontation with an angry *Girl of the Night*. "I'm not looking for female company."

"You want a boy? I could arrange that."

"No boy, either. I'm meeting someone. Maybe another time."

Her fingers held his sleeve. "For a ten-credit note I'll let you pass without screaming *rape*." Her eyes glowed softly in her painted face. *Glowdust* did that to a person. And she was high on it.

He pulled out a five-credit note and handed it to her. "That's all I can spare. Things are slow right now."

She ripped the money from his fingers and stuffed it into the cleavage of her ample breasts. "I'll take it," she said, smiling sweetly. "You're a fool, you know. I can tell you've never been down here. For ten credits I would have given you the best pussy you ever had."

"I guess I'm a fool," he said, walking away.

"Take my advice," she called after him. "Don't pay more than ten. Boys cost you twenty."

The girl's laughter taunted him. He tuned it out, pushed open the door into Serpent's Fang. Loud music washed over him. On a dance floor, couples twisted their bodies into grotesque angles. He had never been one for dancing; had never learned how.

The music sounded wrong in his ears. There seemed to be no melody, only drumming and pulsating strings. It vibrated through his body like an electric shock. He knew he wouldn't be able to stay long, unless he took one of the various drugs available from the bar. Already he was beginning to get a nauseating feeling in the pit of his stomach.

Nathan had told him that Yan Yamoto was a regular at Serpent's Fang and known there. He had a description of the man, but with so many patrons in the club it was easy for him to get lost in the crowd.

Houston fought his way through the dancing couples and made it to the bar without being accosted by one of the *Serpent-dancers*; girls who had their naked bodies painted with tiny fluorescent scales, giving them the appearance of giant snakes.

A number of men and women sat at the bar. Some nursed their drinks, while others watched the people on the dance floor. He saw one couple at the end of the bar locked in a deep kiss, the man's hand buried under woman's blouse, fondling her breasts.

Another couple sat close to each other. The man held a glass filled with an amber liquid. Both people had a thin tube dipped into the glass. Their eyes were closed as they sipped from the liquid.

Houston didn't have to guess what they were drinking. He had tried it only once and wished he hadn't. Angel tears. It put the user into a state of ecstasy for hours and provided incredible stamina. It was also highly addictive. It had taken him months of agony to rid his mind of the desire to use it again. Lucky for him, he was deep in the jungle searching for emeralds with no way of acquiring the drug.

It was a popular drug because it had no side effects, other than keeping the user a hostage of his desire to use it again.

Searching for a vacated stool he didn't see one, but he managed to squeeze into an empty spot and signaled the bartender, who was busy mixing drinks. "I'm looking for a man," he shouted.

She gave him a sour look. "Aren't we all?"

He pushed a five-credit note in her direction. "His name is Yan Yamoto. He's about five ten, around one hundred-sixty pounds. Scar over his left eye."

She eyed him suspiciously. Then she bent across the counter. "Is he a friend of yours?"

"No. I don't even know him."

"What do you want him for?"

Looking at her painted lips he could see the tiny needle marks in her lower lip where she had injected aging-inhibitors. She looked young but from close up it was obvious she had seen better days. Years ago.

She finished mixing the drinks and walked away to hand them to the people who had ordered them. Then she came back. Leaning close, she said, "I'll take you to him. It'll cost you another five."

He gave her the money and wondered how much it would cost him until he finally made contact with Yamato. He followed her into the back, down a corridor. She stopped in front of a door.

"In there."

Houston grabbed her arm, suddenly suspicious and cautious. "I won't be robbed in there or worse?"

She stared into his eyes. "No. Unless you play it stupid. Enjoy yourself."

He let go of her and watched her walk away. Taking the gun out of his jacket pocket, he shoved it behind his back into his belt.

His hands felt clammy. The music from the dance floor sounded subdued, but the drums seemed to have transferred into his chest, keeping rhythm with the pounding of his heart.

Squaring his shoulders, he opened the door. The unmistakable sweet odor of *Lucid Mist* hung heavy in the air. He took a deep breath and walked into the room, nearly stumbling over a couple on the floor. A man lay between a woman's open thighs, her legs locked behind his back. They lay without moving, lost in a world of sexual ecstasy.

They could stay like that for hours until the effects of the drug wore off. Another couple lay not far from them in a similar position.

Against a wall in the back, a row of chairs was occupied by lone men and women, strapped into their seats. They sat with slack faces, seemingly unconscious. While their bodies sat rigid, unresponsive to external stimuli, their minds were roaming dream worlds of their own choosing.

Houston had never taken *Lucid Mist*, but he knew a woman who had been a user. She died after spending a week of continuous unsupervised injections, not drinking or eating during that time.

Getting drugs was easy. There was no law forbidding use or possession, but users who valued their life and sanity never used drugs when alone. Most came to places like Serpent's Fang where they would be under strict supervision and safe from molestation while their bodies were vulnerable.

At least that was the assumption, but no one was ever quite safe on Epsilon, not even in a so-called civilized place like Epsilon City.

He spotted the man he was searching for in one of the seats. Stepping over the couple on the floor, he headed in his direction, when a voice from behind him made him stop.

"Where do you think you're going?"

Houston turned to look for the man who had spoken. He found him standing beside a bunk, pulling up his pants.

When Houston looked into the bunk, he saw the naked body of a woman lying prone on the soft cushion. Her face was drooping. She'd wake up unaware she had been sexually assaulted by the man who was supposed to keep her from being harmed.

Houston casually put his hand behind his back, touching his gun. "I'm checking up on a friend. We were supposed to meet in front."

"Well, I guess he decided he couldn't wait for you." The man grinned, casually closing the front of his shirt. He turned his head and looked at the woman in the bunk. "Go ahead, have some fun while you wait for your friend to come out of it. She won't mind."

"But I mind." A wave of anger welled up inside Houston. He felt like taking his gun and shoving it between the man's white teeth.

The man laughed. "Come on, don't act so moral. Just the fact you are here tells me you are looking for some form of entertainment. These women come here because they're lonely, seeking pleasure. I provide that. I make real what they dream of. It enhances their pleasure." He grimaced. "And mine."

He gave Houston a sly look. "Normally I charge five credits for it, but I'll let you have her for two." His gaze wandered to another bunk. "Or take her. She's young and beautiful. I tried her out the first time she was here and found her quite satisfying. This is only her second time in this place. She's practically a virgin."

Houston cringed inside and forced his mind to calm down. He even managed to smile. "No thanks, I'll take a rain check. Maybe next time."

The man shrugged. "Suit yourself. They're not always this good-looking." His eyes fixed on Houston. "Which one is your friend?"

Houston pointed. "That one. Yan Yamoto. How long has he been under?"

"A couple of hours. He's won't wake up for at least another couple."

"Damn! I don't feel like hanging around that long. Is there nothing you can do?"

"I could give him a shot, but he won't be happy. They get cranky when you pull them out of their little worlds like that. Besides, he's paid for the whole experience." The man hesitated. "I don't feel like messing with him. Do you know who he is?"

"Of course I do. Why do you think I want to talk to him?"

The man's eyebrows went up. "Are you a member? You don't look like one of them."

"I'm not. This is strictly business."

"I hope you know who you're dealing with."

Houston laughed. It came out cruel and almost condescending. "I hope *he* knows who he is dealing with." He didn't miss the man's reaction and pressed on. "My people won't be happy if I don't deliver."

"Your people?"

"That's right. My people." He smiled, not knowing where he was going with that. "Best you don't get involved, my friend. The less you know the healthier you'll stay."

The man lifted both hands. "You've never been here. How can I help you?"

"Give him the antidote. I'd like to take him out of here. Sober."

It only took a few minutes before Yamoto began to stir. He opened his eyes and stared unseeing at Houston. Slowly, the light of life began to flicker in his eyes, but he was still living in a world only he could see.

With the help of the other man, Houston pulled Yamoto out of his seat and draped the young man's arm around his shoulder. "Is there an empty room I could put him in until he's coming around?"

The man nodded, suddenly eager to help. "Come on, I'll show you."

Houston nearly dragged Yamoto with him. The room the other man showed him, was small, a storage room, but it would do. "Thanks, friend. Say, what's your name?"

"York. My name is York."

"You've been helpful. I won't forget."

"I'd better get back. Tell your people I hope everything works out.

Any time you'll need someone to help out, I'll be here." He turned and almost stumbled away in his eagerness.

Houston wiped the sweat from his brow. "Next time I might just put a bullet into your brain, you sick bastard," he murmured.

He locked the door leading into the storage room and watched his prisoner slowly coming back to awareness. Yamoto took a sudden deep breath and stared around him. "Where the hell am I?" His eyes fell on Houston. "Who are you?"

"Who do you want me to be?" Houston countered.

Yamoto's slanted eyes became narrow slits. "What do you want from me?" He didn't wait for an answer. His fist shot out and narrowly missed Houston's head.

Houston punched him in the belly. Then he pulled his gun and shoved it under Yamoto's chin. "I'll splatter your brains all over this room if you try that again," he said harshly.

"Do you know who I am?" Yamoto gave him a defiant look.

"You are a member of the turdfeeders who kidnapped a friend of mine. Don't try to impress me."

Yamoto laughed. "I don't believe you know what you're getting yourself into. Nobody messes with us. Nobody. You are dead! Do you understand?"

Houston smiled grimly. "Your threat doesn't scare me, turd. I'm the one with the gun. I am going to ask you a few questions. Should I not be satisfied with your answers I'll put a bullet into you."

"You wouldn't dare! My friends will revenge me."

"Let me worry about that. Maybe I should give you a sample of what you can expect? I'll start with your right foot." Houston put one hand around Yamoto's throat and aimed his gun at the man's foot.

Yamoto struggled in his grip and Houston tightened his digging fingers.

"All right." Yamoto choked. He gasped for air when Houston eased up on the pressure. "What do you want to know?"

"Where did they take the girl?"

"Which girl?"

"The one your friends kidnapped. She's got red hair."

"I know nothing about that," Yamoto protested.

"I didn't ask if you were involved. I want to know where they would take her."

"Probably into the den."

"The den? Is that supposed to be funny?"

"No. That's what we call our meeting place."

"I guess it is fitting. What else would rats call it? And where is this den?"

Yamoto hesitated and Houston dug his fingers into the man's throat. "If I tell you I'll sign my own death sentence."

"You'll sign it for sure if you don't tell me," Houston said with a growl. "Start talking. Time is running out." It was hot in the confinement of the storage room, and he was beginning to sweat. He didn't know how long he could keep up the pressure until Yamoto would fight back in earnest. As tough as he made himself sound, he wasn't certain he could shoot the other man in cold blood.

"Nobody knows about the place but us," Yamoto said. "We are safe there."

"And where is this secret place?" Houston pressed the gun into Yamoto's neck again. "I'm getting impatient and jittery."

"It is below the city. Underground. We found it by accident."

"Take me there. Now!"

"Are you stupid? You'll never get back alive."

"Another problem you needn't worry about. Let's go." He moved the barrel of the gun and forced it between Yamoto's ribs. Then he opened the door and pushed the other man into the corridor.

Yamoto grinned. "You *are* stupid. The only way out of here is through the bar. I have friends in there. You'll leave this place a dead man." He winced when Houston pushed harder.

"You'll be dead long before me. Walk slowly, smile, act as if you and I are the best of friends and don't try to do any heroic deeds."

At that moment, a door opened, and York stepped out. He smiled when he saw Houston and Yamoto. "I see your associate is back with the living," he said.

Yamoto tensed and opened his mouth. Houston gave the gun a twist, letting it dig into Yamoto's back. "Not for long if he doesn't smarten up," he said, chuckling. "We had a nice chat and I think we've come to an understanding." He winked. "Everything all right in there?"

York grinned. "You should take some time off and try out the new one who just came in." He made a motion with his hand. "She's hotter than hell's inferno. I'll let you be the first."

A furious hatred for the man exploded inside Houston and it took all his self-control not to burn him where he stood. He forced his lips into a smile. "Thanks, York. I appreciate the offer. Don't worry I won't forget this. Maybe some day I can give you what you deserve." He gave Yamoto a push. "But now we must move on. My business can't wait."

He knew York was watching them, but he didn't give in to the urge to turn and look back. When they opened the door that led into the bar area, a wave of noisy music and laughter spilled into the corridor. He closed the door behind him and pushed Yamoto ahead of him.

He saw the bartender looking at him and waved to her, giving her a friendly smile. She returned the gesture and went back to mixing her drinks. They made it through the dancing crowd without any incidents, and Houston let out his breath with a *whoosh* when they finally walked through the main door into the corridor outside, leaving the noise and merriment of Serpent's Fang behind.

Yamoto tried one last time to make a dash for freedom, but Houston clamped his hand around the man's arm, while keeping the gun pressed into his side. "So far, you've done well. Let's not spoil our achievement," he said with a low voice. "You can die as easily out here than in there."

He looked around and was relieved not to see the two *Girl's of the Night*. Either they found their customers or decided to call it quits for the evening. "Where is your scooter?" he asked.

"Parked in the public area. Where else?" Yamoto said with defiance, but he walked meekly in front of Houston as they headed for the main road.

As it turned out, Houston's scooter wasn't far away from Yamoto's. "Drive ahead of me. I'll follow you." He stared grimly at the other man. "Forget any notion of outrunning me. I'm used to riding a scooter and I'm a crack shot with my gun. I've had a lot of practice. Nothing would please me more than shooting you while you're racing down these corridors."

"What are you going to do when we get there?"

"One thing at a time. Let's get there first. Now, go!"

He had no illusions. Yamoto would try to loose him. However, he had no choice but to let him take the lead. He couldn't afford the chance of having Yamoto sit behind him on his scooter. He'd be too vulnerable. Or he could sit behind Yamoto. An option he considered only briefly and dismissed it. He'd have to hang onto the other man. It wouldn't be too difficult for Yamoto to lose his unwanted passenger.

Yamoto took off with a wild dash and began racing down the road, but Houston had anticipated it. He stayed as close as possible to the other man's scooter without putting both of them in danger. They had to watch oncoming traffic and also other riders going in the same direction. A couple of times they overtook scooters who seemed to be on a joyride, cruising in slow speed down the main corridor.

When they reached the lowest level, Yamoto took a narrow side corridor and followed it until suddenly there were no more minisuns embedded in the ceiling, leaving the corridor in darkness.

The scooters were equipped with lights and the darkness wasn't a problem. Houston noticed that the air didn't smell as fresh as on the upper levels. A musky odor became prevalent the further they traveled. The corridor began to run in a straight line, away from the city tower but descending steadily.

A light glowed suddenly ahead and became brighter as they neared it.

The corridor ended inside a large cavern. Stalactites hung down from the high ceiling like dark fingers reaching for the intruders. Someone had installed a number of minisuns on some of the stalactites. They threw long shadows, lending the place an aura of unreality.

From the wet floor, thick stalagmites grew toward the ceiling, many of them touching the glistening cones who invaded their territory from above.

Yamoto maneuvered his scooter through the obstacle course with great skill, dodging around the stalagmites in wide circles, once in a while doubling back. He was trying hard to leave Houston behind and possibly lost in the unfamiliar expanse of the underworld they traveled, but Houston was determined not to let Yamoto get away.

The chase ended abruptly when Yamoto stopped his scooter in front of a wall as sheer and smooth as a sheet of black ice.

He grinned at Houston. "Welcome to the Den. This is where we part company."

He pushed his scooter toward the wall.

Then he was gone.

[3]

HOUSTON STARED AT THE BLANK WALL, LOOKING FOR AN ENTRANCE. Getting off his scooter, he walked the length of the wall. He touched it with a flat hand. It felt warm to the touch. A slight tingling ran through his hand, like a gentle burst of static electricity.

The wall was smooth without any breaks. It melded into the rough stone on either side and on the floor. When he looked up, he discovered the same at the top.

Son-of-a-bitch! Where had Yamoto gone? He couldn't have just walked through the wall.

Houston ran his hands across the wall where Yamoto had last stood.

As smooth as polished glass.

Yamoto had outfoxed him.

Angry at his own stupidity, he searched for a rock and threw it at the wall. A metallic clang rang through the cavern as the missile hit the wall and bounced off to roll across the rough ground.

The metallic sound told Houston that the wall was not a natural phenomenon but had been built by someone. Certainly not the Tunnel Rats.

The Uur? He didn't believe so. They didn't work metal because

41

they didn't have the technology. That left either an ancient civilization or someone from another planet.

The miners discovered ruins, evidence that reptilian races once lived on Epsilon, but those had been ruins, nothing like this. He heard rumors about discoveries of ancient Spider artifacts and ruins resembling Spider habitats.

He walked once more the length of the wall, but still, no way to get through it. He hunkered down, waited, hoping either Yamoto might make an appearance or one of the other members of the Tunnel Rats.

After waiting for hours, he made a decision and climbed onto his scooter. This needed to be reported to the authorities. Who knew what dangers lay waiting behind that wall? Suddenly he was afraid for Tara's safety.

He found his way back through the cavern easy enough. All he had to do was follow the minisuns. Once he was in the tunnel, he had no trouble getting back into the city. Since it was close to morning and he was tired, he went home and tried to catch a few hours of rest but didn't sleep much.

In the afternoon, he headed for Security Headquarters.

When he parked his scooter, he noticed a black, armored vehicle squatting like a huge ugly predator in the parking lot but didn't give it much thought. He walked through the door with the sign over it and entered the front office of Epsilon City Security.

The same uniformed clerk who had been there when he and Tara were apprehended sat behind the desk. His eyes widened in recognition when he saw Houston. "Whatever it is you want, you are not coming at a good time," he said.

Houston grinned crookedly. "Is there ever a good time to come to Security?"

"Believe me, today really is not a good day. Epsilon City Security has been taken over by some military dictator. He fired the Chief and replaced him with a stranger. I don't think there is ever going to be a good day again." The man sounded resigned. He turned his head and looked at the door as someone pushed it open and repeated, "Not a good day."

Houston followed his gaze and watched a group of black-clad, armed men, carrying flash rifles ready to be fired, pushing their way through the door.

"We're looking for Commodore Chelzic," one of them barked.

The Security man pointed at the door beside the desk. "Through there."

Houston didn't have to ask the Security man who those men were. A small shiver ran through his body. Union Troopers always spelled trouble. Something big was brewing and he didn't care to think about that.

"It might not be convenient today," he said, "but the young lady who was with me last time I was here, she is in trouble. And there is..."

He stopped talking when the door into the back offices opened and the Troopers came back again. This time there was a large man with them. He was dressed in a camouflage outfit and had *Military* written all over him. He threw a curious glance at Houston as he walked by, but then they all disappeared into the corridor outside.

"That was...?"

The Security man nodded. "That was Commodore Chelzic. Apparently, we are under Marshall Law right now. Whatever that means."

"Who did you say was in charge now?"

"His name is Stonewall. Better call him Chief Stonewall."

Houston sighed. "If he looks like that Commodore, I don't expect much help from him. Is it all right if I try my luck?"

"Go right ahead. Somebody will direct you to him."

When he entered the main office, he saw most of the Security people standing in a group, listening to a big man in a Scout's uniform. Two of the black-clad Troopers stood on either side of him, flash rifles in hand. Another man, quite tall but lanky, also wearing the Scout's uniform, stood slightly to the side.

"...I don't like it any more than you people do," the big man said. "I didn't volunteer for this job, but since I've been put into this position, I expect everyone to accept me as the new Chief of Security. I came here as Master Scout Stonewall, but you will address me as Chief Stonewall."

Houston studied the man while he spoke. He was tall, over six feet, with a large frame, weighing at least two hundred pounds. Not as tall and bulky as the Commodore, but still presenting an imposing figure. The fact that he didn't look as grim and cold as the Commodore, gave Houston hope he may be amiable to talk to.

The two Union Troopers were another story. They did not convey friendliness. Their watchful eyes seemed to be everywhere. He knew they already spotted him and marked as a possible threat to the new Chief since he was a new equation in their assessment of the situation.

He waited until Chief Stonewall finished talking and had gone through the door behind him before he made his way through the desks toward the Chief's office.

The Troopers barred his way when he approached the door to the office. "State your reason for being here," one of them barked with a cold and demanding voice.

"I need to talk to the Chief about a kidnapping and something important I have discovered." Houston refused to be intimidated.

"Chief Stonewall is busy at the moment. Talk to one of the Security men."

"What I have to tell is meant only for someone in a position of command. Someone who can make a quick decision. This matter is too important to be discussed with a lower clerk." Even though he was seething inside, he kept his voice level and controlled. He had dealt with the Military before and knew that soldiers were sometimes pigheaded about following protocol. He had no time for playing games, but he couldn't afford to be brushed off. He looked up at the Trooper. "You don't want to be reprimanded for dragging your feet when it comes to the security of this planet, do you?"

"What is going on here?"

The Trooper turned when he heard the Chief's voice. "This man insists on seeing you, sir."

Houston stepped around the Trooper, who blocked his view. "The security of the city, possibly the whole planet, maybe at stake here, Chief Stonewall. It is of utmost urgency I talk with you... now."

The Chief nodded after a brief hesitation. "Okay, come into my office." Before he walked through the door he told the Troopers, "Don't worry about my safety. I can take care of myself if need be. And I don't believe this man came here to assassinate me."

Houston waited until Stonewall walked behind his desk before he followed him.

"Have a seat and then tell me what this is all about." The Chief pointed at one of the two wooden chairs in front of his desk.

Houston took it gratefully and studied the man who replaced Chief Moore. "So you are the new Chief of Epsilon City's Security."

"Yes, I am, but I don't believe you came here to tell me that."

"Of course not. I can tell by your uniform that you are a Scout. Most likely you are not familiar with Epsilon City. Does the name 'Tunnel Rats' mean anything to you?"

"No."

"Well, they are a bunch of criminals. Young men who roam the tunnels of Epsilon City on their scooters and harass innocent citizens." Houston wiped his hand across his perspiring face, pausing for a moment. "A few days ago, a young lady by the name of Tara Turner came to me for help. She had just arrived on Epsilon and had no place to go, so I let her stay in my apartment." He paused again, slightly embarrassed by what he seemed to be implying, his eyes on the Chief's face. "Until she found a more permanent place."

"I understand Mr...?"

"Houston. David Houston." He stared at Stonewall, his face hot. "I don't believe you do, because there is nothing going on between me and Miss Turner."

"I didn't say that."

"No, you didn't, but I can see in your eyes what you are thinking."

"Are you a mind reader, Mr. Houston?" The Chief's smile seemed to mock him.

"No but it is obvious that you assume...never mind. That is really irrelevant. It doesn't matter what you think. Four days ago, the Tunnel Rats attacked us. They beat me unconscious and kidnapped

Miss Turner. I found their hiding place, but I have no way of getting into it."

"Why did you take this long to report the kidnapping?"

"I needed to recover from my beating, and I wanted to find them myself."

"Why? What were you going to do once you found them? One man against how many...?"

"I never gave it much thought. I just wanted to find her." Houston lifted his shoulders and spread his hands. "To be honest...I didn't expect to get much help from Security. So far, they haven't done anything about the problem we have with the Tunnel Rats."

"Then why come for help now?"

"Because I found something that defies explanation. In the caverns underneath Epsilon City."

"How about giving me a hint."

"They might possibly be ruins of an ancient civilization."

"Interesting." Chief Stonewall touched his wristband; his eyes seemed unfocused for a moment. "Peters, I'd like to see you in my office."

A moment later the door opened, and the lanky man Houston had seen before, walked in. "What is it, Chief?"

Stonewall smiled thinly and shook his head. "Cut the crap, Peters. You don't have to call me Chief."

Peters grinned. "But you are the new Chief of Security. With the position comes the title. Better get used to it. Or would you prefer if I called you Mayor Stonewall?"

"I won't even comment on that." Stonewall shook his head again, seemingly in annoyance, but Houston sensed a certain camaraderie between the two men.

Peters pulled the other chair in the room closer with his foot and sank into it. Looking at Houston, he asked, "Who are you?"

"That is Mr. Houston," Stonewall answered before Houston could introduce himself. "Apparently, he discovered ancient ruins underneath this city."

"Fascinating." Peters didn't seem too impressed. "I think right now we have larger problems than the dead leftovers of an ancient civilization."

"These *leftovers* don't appear to be dead, Scout Peters, and I have reason to believe a friend of mine is held prisoner behind a wall of metal that seems impenetrable. I think there is a secret door to get into the room behind the wall." Houston was getting impatient. He didn't have any illusion about getting any help from Security, even with the new Chief. It seemed he had his own problems to deal with.

"A secret door," Peters said with a tiny smile. "That has such an ominous sound to it."

An angry impulse flashed through Houston. He didn't need to be patronized. "Please, do not try to humor me by analyzing what I'm telling you. There is no time to be lost. A young woman's life is in danger, and she needs our help. I promised her protection and I failed her miserably." He rose in his chair. "If you won't help, I'll have to seek it elsewhere."

"Take it easy, Mr. Houston." The Chief waved his hand, indicating for Houston to sit down again. "We didn't say we weren't going to help you, but you must understand my position. I just inherited a job I never wanted. I am not familiar with this city and the people who inhabit it. So give me some slack, all right? What makes you think those ruins are not dead?"

"Because I saw a man disappear right in front of my eyes. One moment he was there, the next he was gone."

Stonewall's eyes flickered to Peters. "That doesn't sound like whatever Mr. Houston found is dead. Is it possible that the Uur are technically more advanced than they admit?"

"No. The Uur or anyone else on this planet don't have the technology. By that I mean the indigenous population. Whatever is underneath this city belongs to someone else. Either to the Dragons or the Spiders. If it still works, we may have a potential threat." Peters seemed show some sudden concern. "I suggest we check it out."

Stonewall nodded. "I agree, but we need to keep it quiet. We don't want to create a panic. You and I and the two Troopers will accompany Mr. Houston."

"When?"

"Now."

Houston drew in a breath of relief. Perhaps he had misjudged this Stonewall.

"We will need transportation," the Chief said. "What are you driving, Mr. Houston?"

"A scooter. Only large enough for two people."

"Security has larger vehicles. We'll have to request one without anyone asking questions."

"You don't have to ask for permission. You are the Chief, remember?" Peters chuckled. Houston didn't really see the humor in his remark.

As they walked out of the Chief's office, Stonewall told the two Troopers to come with them.

Sitting in the backseat of the scooter, Houston gave Peters, who sat in the driver's seat, directions. It seemed to take an eternity driving through the cavern with the stalactites, but they finally found the place where Yamoto and his scooter disappeared.

After walking the length of the metal wall, Stonewall stood gazing at the shiny barrier. Then he put his hand on the smooth surface. "It feels warm," he said. "You were correct, Mr. Houston, whatever this is it is not dead."

"I believe that the Tunnel Rats are hiding behind this wall. And they have Miss Turner with them," Houston said.

"But how did they get beyond this barrier?"

"They teleported?" Peters suggested.

"Nobody possesses that technology. Not even the Spiders."

"As far as we know. Even if they did, they would never share it with anyone." Peters also touched the wall. "I am detecting a slight vibration. Where exactly did you see that man disappear, Mr. Houston?"

"Right about where you are standing, Scout Peters."

Peters walked a few steps but kept his hand on the wall. He walked back and forth a few times. "The vibrations seem to be stronger in this area," Peters said.

"If your theory is correct then that is where the portal must be." Stonewall stood stroking his chin. "How do you activate it?"

"By sending some kind of a signal?"

"That would suggest a remote device. The man must have carried it on his person."

"I remember he had an ancient looking medallion hanging from a chain around his neck. Could that have been the device?" Houston tried to recall what it looked like and then he suddenly remembered something. He nodded eagerly. "Yes, you could be right. They all wore them around their necks. Each one of those youths who accosted us had one. I assumed they were jewelry."

"Well, we don't have one. Maybe we can blast our way in," Peters said.

Stonewall seemed to agree. He looked at the Troopers. "See if you can cut a hole into this wall."

The Troopers nodded. Stepping back, they aimed their flash rifles at the wall. After spraying it with bursts of pure energy, the wall showed no signs of stress.

"It is useless." The Chief stared at the wall. "That leaves us with only one option. We will have to intercept either one or all of them. They'll have to come out sooner or later. For now, we'll leave in case they have the means to see us."

Houston didn't like the idea, but he knew they had no choice.

Stonewall left both troopers stationed in the corridor. They objected to his decision. "Our job is to protect you," one of them said.

"I appreciate that," the Chief told them. "But my safety comes second to the safety of Epsilon. This whole planet may be threatened by what lies behind this wall."

Houston agreed. There was nothing they could do at the moment. He couldn't shake the feeling of dread and he was angry for being so helpless.

———

Two hours later Houston received a call from Scout Peters that the Troopers had taken a couple of the Tunnel Rats into custody. He rushed down to Security Headquarters.

The two Troopers were waiting in the tunnel. The Tunnel Rats with them didn't look happy.

One of them opened his painted lips and pushed out a split tongue. Houston recognized him immediately. "You'll never find your beautiful lady, Davy. Are you still so angry, Davy?" He spoke with a singing, mocking voice, his split tongue lending it a slight lisp.

Houston pushed past Stonewall to confront the man who mocked him. "If you harmed her in any way, I swear I'll kill you, you freak!" he said through his teeth, his fists pulled back to hit the man in the face.

"Let us handle this, Mr. Houston." The Chief pulled Houston away from the grinning youth and turned to the Tunnel Rat. "We have no time to play games. I'm only going to ask once. What is behind that wall at the end of the cavern and how are we going to get behind it?"

"Go fuck a lizard!" Sneering, the youth spit into Stonewall's face.

Stonewall backhanded him. Houston was happy to see the split lip Stonewall's hand left behind.

Wiping the blood from his mouth, the youth spat again. Then he pushed out his forked tongue and made a warbling sound. His friend joined him in his act of defiance.

"Make them talk," Stonewall said calmly to one of the Troopers. He turned to Houston. "Is he one of the ones who kidnapped your friend?"

Houston nodded. "He is one of them. I'll never forget his ugly face. Let me have a go at him."

Stonewall shook his head. "Can't do that. You're a civilian. Let the professionals handle it. It won't be long before they're going to spill their guts. Literally, if necessary."

He gave the two Troopers the go-ahead sign. "Give them a few minutes," he told Peters and Houston. "There is no need for any of us to watch this."

Houston hated violence but this was one occasion where he would have liked to help with the interrogation. When he heard the moaning sounds and screams of the two Tunnel Rats, he didn't feel any pity with them. They deserved whatever they received.

"Are you sure that is necessary?" one of the Security men asked, obviously not agreeing with the Chief's decision.

Stonewall nodded and said, "If we want to achieve our objective it is."

"What is our objective?" the other Security man asked.

"To rescue a young woman and to make certain there is no danger to this planet hiding beneath Epsilon City."

"The Tunnel Rats are nothing but a bunch of over-zealous young men creating a nuisance for the citizens, but they are certainly no danger to Epsilon." When another scream echoed through the tunnel, the Security man turned to look back. "There is really no need to torture them."

"They are criminals," Houston shouted angrily. "The security in this city is at best laughable. You people have no problem harassing an innocent young woman who committed one small oversight, but you won't take these vermin off the street!"

"If they commit an offence we will arrest them, until then we have no reason to waste valuable recourses chasing unsubstantiated rumors." Even though the officer spoke calmly, Houston sensed his apprehension and subdued annoyance.

"We are able to proceed." One of the Troopers came toward them and waved with one hand.

The two youths lay motionless on the ground. Houston wondered if they were dead. "They are alive," the Trooper said as if reading Houston's mind. "But they may need to seek medical help."

"Will they be all right if we leave them here for a while?" The Chief asked.

"They will be in pain, but otherwise they'll be fine." The Trooper didn't seem concerned.

"Good. Then let us carry on. Do you have the means to get past the barrier?"

The Trooper held up one of the chains the youths had been wearing around their necks. A medallion was attached to it. "This is the key," he said.

"Did you get instructions how to use it?"

The Trooper nodded. "We did."

The Chief regarded the Tunnel Rats for a moment. "I don't want to leave them here. Put them into the vehicle. Peters and Mr. Houston...hitch a ride with the Security men. We don't have far to go."

Leaving the dark tunnel behind, they entered the large cavern. The Stalactites and stalagmites looked as foreboding as before.

When they reached the wall, one of the Troopers held the medallion against the wall. He disappeared from sight as if he had never existed. Just like Yamoto.

The other Trooper attempted to follow him, but Stonewall held him back. "No. We don't know what's on the other side. Let's find out how we all can pass through." He walked to the Security vehicle. "How can you transfer more than one person through that wall?" he asked the two miserable looking Tunnel Rats.

"Fuck you!"

"I can have my man work you over a little bit more," Stonewall told them with a brittle voice. "Maybe we can spare us a trip to the hospital."

Houston wished he would follow through with his threat, but they needed to know how they all could get to the other side.

"I'll tell you," one of them said.

"All right. I'm waiting."

"If you let me out, I'll show you."

"Traitor," the other one shouted.

"I don't want to die. You can do what you want, Trevor. I'm done with this shit anyway." Houston watched him as he got off his seat, moving slowly, obviously in pain. Moaning, he stepped out of the car and stood swaying. "I think I'm going to be sick," he said.

Stonewall grabbed his arm. "Save it for later. Now...tell us how it's done."

"It is quite simple. All you have to do is stay in a tight cluster while one of you touches the wall with the medallion." He tried to smile but only managed a pained grimace. Houston didn't feel any pity for him. "Can you give me something for the pain? Please."

Stonewall regarded him for a moment. "What's your name?"

"Sel."

"Okay, Sel. You've been helpful. Maybe not all is lost with you."

"I promise if you help me out of this, I'll quit the Tunnel Rats. They're a bunch of losers anyway." Sel gave him a hopeful look.

Stonewall handed him something. "Here, chew on this. It will ease the pain."

Sel took it eagerly and put it into his mouth. "Thank you, sir. I won't forget this. One more thing. If I help you, will you go easy on me? Can you promise me that?"

"I'll promise." Stonewall waved to the Security guard who had been driving the vehicle. "Stay with the prisoner and guard him." Turning back to the others, he said, "All right, let's all stay close together. Keep your eyes open and weapons ready." His eyes fell on Sel. "You're coming with us. It better work."

[4]

As soon as the Trooper touched the medallion to the wall, a slight tingling went through Houston and then he found himself on the other side of the wall. Chief Stonewall and the others were right beside him. The Trooper who had stepped through the barrier first, stood nearby, his weapon leveled at a group of men. They stood with arms raised above their heads. One lay on the ground, his body in a heap, a gun in his hand. Houston guessed by the way he lay that he was probably dead.

"I was beginning to wonder if you could make it through," the Trooper said.

"We did have a slight holdup, but we are here now." Chief Stonewall said, his eyes raking the men lined up against one wall. "Were you going to shoot them all?" he asked.

"Just about," the Trooper growled. "They are unwilling to cooperate."

"Where is the girl?" Houston shouted at the Tunnel Rats, hating them as they stood there in their flashy clothes; large, golden hoops hanging from their earlobes, their lips and eyes painted with loud colors, like a bunch of old women in a pathetic attempt to recapture their lost youthful beauty. They could have been a pitiful lot, had it not been for their shaved heads, their tattoos, and the chains around their necks. It made them look menacing and disgusting.

Stonewall glanced at him. "Take it easy, friend. One step at a time."

"Every moment we waste puts her in deeper danger," Houston said, clenching his fists to keep his anger under control.

"It's *Angry Davy*," one of the Tunnel Rats sneered.

"Angry Davy...Angry Davy..." they chanted.

"Tell them to shut up!" Houston snarled.

Stonewall stared at the chanting youths. "You heard the man," he said sharply.

They laughed. "He's no man. He let us take his girlfriend with his lizard tucked between his legs," one shouted.

"That's enough!" Stonewall thundered. "Now I'm asking you the same question. Where is the girl?"

"She's with the others." The speaker chuckled. "And the others." They all laughed.

"I can show you," Sel said behind them.

One of the Tunnel Rats stepped forward. He glared at Stonewall. "Your ape-man murdered one of my friends. I will take that up with Security. Besides, you are trespassing. This is our domain. Nobody is allowed here without special permission. Our permission." He pointed a finger at Sel. "We'll deal with you, traitor. You are a dead man!"

"You are in no position to threaten anyone," Stonewall told him with an icy voice that sent shivers down even Houston's back. "If you have a complaint, you can tell me right now. I am the new Chief of Security. You are all under arrest."

"You can't arrest us." The youth who spoke looked at the Chief with a defiant expression. "We are citizens of Epsilon city. We have rights like everyone else."

Houston wanted to say something but kept his mouth shut. He looked at Stonewall, who glared at the speaker with cold eyes. "The only rights you have are the ones I allow you. You are misfits of society, who prey on upstanding citizens. By being members of a gang makes you criminals in my eyes. I might just decide to have you all shot. It will save us all a lot of trouble and expense." Turning to Sel, he said, "All right. Now earn your freedom. Where is the girl?"

Sel pointed to the back of the room. "Follow me, please."

Before they followed Sel, Stonewall told one of the Security men, "Call for a prison wagon. Then disarm the prisoners and make sure you get all of the keys. We don't want them escaping. If one resists or tries to make a run for it, shoot him." He turned away. "Mr. Peters and Mr. Houston, please accompany us."

The other Trooper tried to go with them, but Stonewall shook his head. "Stay with the prisoners. I don't trust them. They are desperate, with nothing to loose. If I find I need you, I'll call you."

They walked past strange looking machines. When Houston looked at them, he felt nauseated and a strange twisting inside his mind. A narrow corridor took them into another room, larger than the one they left behind, with more machines and shelves filled with transparent spheres. What Houston saw inside the spheres made him shiver.

"Are those what I think they are?" Peters whispered.

Stonewall nodded. "There is no mistake. We are looking at preserved Spider bodies." His voice conveyed how serious he took what they saw.

"Are you sure they are dead?"

"You're not suggesting they are alive inside those globes?"

"Not alive in that sense. I mean, they could be in stasis. Look at the wires leading to the globes. And those machines, they are still working. Why? For what purpose?"

Stonewall walked to one of the shelves and looked at it with curiosity. Shaking his head, he said, "This doesn't make sense. When did the Spiders built all this?"

"Everything looks almost new, but it can't be. We've been here over twenty years. Somebody was bound to notice Spider activities on Epsilon." Peters touched one of the spheres. Pulling his hand away, he said, "It feels awfully cold and there is definitely some kind of power enveloping the whole thing. I can detect a slight vibration, like static electricity."

"Do you know what this is?" Stonewall looked at the Tunnel Rat.

Sel shrugged. "Like you said, they're Spiders. You'll understand better when you see what I'm going to show you."

Stepping around another machine, they stopped walking. Houston heard Peters cursing violently. At first, he didn't see the reason, but then he saw the transparent barrier and the hairy creatures behind it, crawling over each other.

"Those are young Spiders," he said, feeling cold inside when he recognized the origin of the white bones littering the ground. When he stepped closer to the barrier, the Spiders scuttled toward the transparent wall, sharp mandibles clicking. A small group that had been busy in the back of the room broke apart and rushed to join the others in front of the window. Feeling sick, Houston turned away when he saw the bloody, half-eaten human body that was clearly that of a young woman and cried out in anguish. His stomach heaved and, retching, he bent over.

"I will kill them for this." His voice came out in choked gasps.

When he heard the weak voice of a woman calling, he looked around, faint hope rising in him. Behind one of the machines, he saw a cage. A naked girl clung to the bars and stared at them out of large eyes. She appeared thin, gaunt, like someone who hadn't eaten or slept for days. Her breasts were covered by long, filthy-looking strands of hair. He noticed her thin arms as she stretched them through the bars.

"Please, help me." Her voice sounded dry and hoarse.

"Are you Tara Turner?" Stonewall called to her, but Houston knew it wasn't Tara.

With a shake of her head, she said, "My name is Sherina."

Houston rushed by Stonewall and grabbed the bars of the cage. "That...that body in there...is that Tara?" He was afraid of the answer, but he needed to know.

When she shook her head, he relaxed but only for a moment. "That is..." She covered her face with her hands and let out a series of heart wrenching sobs. Wiping her eyes, she stared at them. "Are you with them?"

"No, we are not with them. We are from Epsilon Security. We'll get you out of here." Stonewall spoke with a soothing voice.

Houston didn't see any tears when the girl began to cry, but her eyes were wide open, and her face twisted into a mask of sorrow and relief.

"I've been praying for a long time." Her voice came out in a whisper. "I never thought my prayers would be answered." She smiled. "I'm not really a religious person." She seemed to realize that she was nude in front of three strange men, because she gasped and tried to cover her pubic area with her hands. "I must look a sight and I'm naked..."

"You look beautiful and don't worry about being naked," Peters said. "You can have my shirt."

"Thank you. You are so kind." She tried to smile but winced and touched her swollen, cracked lips with one hand.

"Stand back," Stonewall said. "We'll have to cut through the bars."

The hole they cut was barely large enough when the girl stumbled through it and into the arms of Peters. As he had promised, he took off his shirt and draped it around her shoulders. Sobbing, she clung to him.

"It's all right," Peters told her in a hoarse voice and put an arm around her shoulder. "You're safe now."

"You were trying to tell us who that girl was inside that room," Stonewall said.

"Her name is...was Helina. She was so scared. Like all of us. I'll never forget her screams."

"How many girls were there?"

"I don't really know." She shrugged. "When I got here there were five girls in this cage with me. They're all dead now."

"So there could have been more?"

She nodded.

"Those bastards! They need to be punished." Peters forced the words through his clenched teeth.

"They will be," Stonewall said, his voice harsh.

"I feel cold," the girl said. She seemed to notice Sel for the first time and gasped. "He is one of them," she cried out, fear back in her face. "You said you were Security..."

"We are," Stonewall assured her. "Has he harmed you in any way?"

"No, not him. I've never seen him in this room."

"That's right," Sel said, his voice urgent. "I would have never touched her or any of the others."

"Did you know about this?" Stonewall pointed at the scrabbling creatures behind the transparent wall.

"I did, but I didn't want any part of it. I told them it wasn't right." He looked at Stonewall, a pleading look in his eyes. "You have to believe me."

"Where is Tara, the last girl you brought here?" Houston asked with a feeling of dread in his stomach.

"I don't know. I assumed she was in here?"

"You assumed? Didn't you see her?" Houston didn't believe him.

"No. Trevor said he wanted to look after her personally."

"Trevor...that's your friend who we caught with you?" Stonewall asked.

He nodded. "That's him, but he is not my friend. I never liked him." Sel spat on the floor. "He's the one who came up with the idea how we could feed those...those creatures."

"Well, we'll give him special treatment, I'll promise," Stonewall growled. "Let's go back. Somebody has to know what happened to Miss Turner."

"What about me?" Sel pulled on Stonewall's sleeve. "Are you still going to keep your promise to me?"

Stonewall regarded him for a moment. "You helped us getting through that wall, but otherwise you haven't given us much."

"I will testify against them. Just don't shoot me, please. I never felt like one of them, anyway. I'll be a good citizen after this, I swear by my dead mother's name."

"We'll see." Stonewall said.

They went back into the front room. The Tunnel Rats watched them with resentful faces.

"Who is the leader of this gang?" Stonewall asked with a hard, cold voice.

One of them lifted his hand. When he spoke, he spoke with a

rebellious voice. "I am the leader. But let me correct you, sir. This is not a gang. We are nothing but a peace-loving Scooter Club."

Houston growled, not believing his ears, while Peters made a sound like an enraged carnosaur.

Pointing at the girl hanging onto Peters, Stonewall asked, "Explain how this girl ended up in a cage and explain to me the creatures behind the transparent wall. Explain the torn, bloody body that had once been a girl named Helina. Explain the bones!" His words came out slowly in an almost dead voice. Houston could feel the chill in the air.

The Tunnel Rat grinned. "We managed to bring those critters back to life. They needed to be fed. Those girls were trash anyway."

Sherina pointed a finger at him and sobbed, "You murdered my brother!"

"He shouldn't have resisted."

"He tried to save me from you. You're not human, you're a beast, an animal. I hate you and if I could I would kill you myself," she screamed. She covered her face with both hands, while her body shook from her loud sobs.

"What is your name?" Chief Stonewall asked.

The young Tunnel Rat drew himself erect. "I am Sirus Kidwai. My father is Ali Kidwai, the Advocate. You can't touch me."

"Well, Sirus Kidway, please rise and stand over there against that wall." Stonewall said with an almost calm voice.

Sirus rose and walked over the wall. Leaning against the wall, he stood wide-legged, a mocking grin on his brown face.

"Do you recognize anyone who was present when they took the other girls into that room?" Stonewall asked Sherina.

She wiped her eyes and looked over the group. Pointing at three of them, she said, "Those. They were the ones who dragged Helina away."

"You are certain?"

"Yes, I am. I will never forget their faces and the way they laughed when those creatures tore Helina to bits."

"Thank you." The Chief stared at the three. "Join your friend over at that wall," he ordered them. He waited until the three stood beside their leader before he said, "We're looking for the last girl that was brought in here. Her name is Tara Turner. Does anyone know what happened to her?"

Nobody spoke. They just stared. A couple of them looked at their leader for help. "Don't look for advice from him, and don't let him intimidate you. He is no threat to anyone," Stonewall told them.

When one of them lifted his hand partially and then dropped it again, Stonewall fixed his eyes on him.

"You! Do you have anything to tell us?"

The youth hesitated. Then he coughed. "You should ask Trevor."

"Trevor? Okay." Stonewall looked at one of the Troopers. "Go, bring in the other prisoner."

The Trooper went to the wall and pressed the medallion he held against it. Houston watched him disappear. When he came back, he brought Trevor with him. Trevor didn't look too healthy; his face was gray and blood covered. The Trooper shoved him into the room and Trevor nearly fell over his own feet.

"Hello, Trevor. How are you feeling?" The Chief didn't show any sympathy for the youth.

"Fuck you!" Trevor cursed, pushing out his forked tongue. "I demand to see a doctor. I'm dying."

Stonewall shook his head. "I'm going to ask you a question. If I like your answer, I might just give you something to ease the pain."

"What do you want to know?" Trevor glared at him with blood-shot eyes.

"Where is the girl you kidnapped?" Stonewall asked.

"She's safe."

"Where?"

"I can't tell you. Not until you make this pain go away. She is my trump card."

"All right. I'll give you something." Stonewall groped around in his pouch.

"Let me at him," Houston growled. "I'll beat it out of him."

"And kill him in the process." Stonewall took a pill from his pouch and handed it to Trevor. Waiting for a moment until the painkiller began to work, he said, "Start talking."

Trevor gave the Chief a calculating look. "One more condition. If I tell you I won't be prosecuted. I'll go free."

Houston was happy to hear Stonewall say, "That is something I can't promise. You committed a crime and need to be punished. Show or tell us where the girl is. If she's safe, then we'll talk again. That's all I can offer you."

"Well...she's not down here."

"Then tell us where she is!"

"In my room."

"He's lying," Houston shouted.

"No, I'm not. It's the truth. I didn't want her to become food. You know...like the others."

"That seems like a noble enough reason," Stonewall said. The mocking undertone didn't escape Houston, who felt like beating the truth out of Trevor.

"We can easily check out if you're telling the truth," Stonewall carried on. "What's your full name and what floor do you live on?"

"Trevor Fullborne. I live on the forty-second floor. Apartment number twenty-seven."

"Anyone else live there?"

"No, I live alone."

Stonewall turned to one of the Security men. "Have someone check it out."

"Aye, aye, sir," the Security man said. "I can't get through from here, though. My signals are blocked."

"Try from the other side of the wall," Stonewall suggested. He turned to Houston. "There is no reason for you to stay here any longer, Mr. Houston. I know you're anxious to find out if your friend is okay. Go with the officer. Take one of the scooters to get to head office. You can accompany the men to Fullborne's apartment."

Houston nodded. "Thank you for your help, Chief Stonewall."

He and the Security man transported through the wall. The officer used his communicator to contact head office. Houston climbed on the scooter and took off, heading for the office of Security.

A couple of officers waited for him already and he joined them in their vehicle. Houston felt jittery and couldn't wait to find out if Tara was all right. When they reached Apartment twenty-seven on the forty-second floor, they found the door locked, but the Security men didn't waste any time trying to jimmy the lock, they just cut it out with a laser to get into the room.

Houston was on the heels of the two officers and the moment he entered the apartment, he called, "Tara...Tara?"

He heard a weak voice calling from the bedroom, recognized Tara's voice and practically ran into the bedroom. She sat on the edge of the bed, naked. When she saw him, she rose and rushed into his arms.

"Dave, oh, Dave," she sobbed under tears. "I knew you'd come."

He held her tight and brushed her hair soothingly. "You're safe now."

A metal band strapped around her ankle tied her to one of the bedposts with a long chain.

One of the Security men produced a laser and cut through the chain. "We'll have the band removed at Headquarters," he said.

They found Tara's clothes and waited until she was dressed. Houston supported her as they walked to the security vehicle, happy and relieved to have her back safely.

[5]

TARA SMILED SHYLY AT HOUSTON. HER RED HAIR WAS DISHEVELED AND dark blotches under her eyes made her look like someone who had slept in the gutter, but to Houston she was the most beautiful sight he had seen in a long time.

"Are you sure you are all right?" he asked for the second time while holding her in his arms.

"I'm fine, Dave. Everything is fine now." She wiped a hand over her eyes.

"I worried about you." He looked into her face. "You don't look fine."

She gave him a little laugh and disengaged herself from his embrace. "I'm as fine as can be. Say, why would you worry about me? We are practically strangers." Her green eyes studied him. "It is sweet of you though. Nobody ever worried about me before."

"It is my fault this happened to you," he said. "I should have protected you."

"There is nothing you could have done, Dave. Don't blame yourself. There were too many of them."

Houston threw an angry look at the two Security men. "If you people would have taken us home in a vehicle that day, this would never have happened. Instead, you let us wander around by ourselves."

"I know nothing about that, Mr. Houston." The Security man turned to Tara. "I need to ask you a couple of questions, Miss Turner. Did Trevor Fullborne do anything to you that might be deemed inappropriate aside from keeping you against your will in his apartment?"

Tara's laugh was strained and shrill. "If forcing himself on me is deemed inappropriate, yes, then he acted that way?"

"Are you saying Trevor Fullborne raped you?"

"That's what I'm saying."

"How often did that incidence take place?"

"How often he raped me?" She put a finger against her chin. "Well, let's see, there was the first time when he took me to his place, the second time an hour later. He left for a few hours. When he came back, he told me he was horny and if I didn't struggle, he would take his time so I could enjoy it also. I didn't struggle, but I sure as hell didn't enjoy it." She closed her eyes and took a deep breath.

"Was that the last time he raped you?"

When she opened her eyes, they were moist. "He raped me twice again that night and two more times during the next day. Or maybe three times. I didn't keep score." She broke into tears and covered her face with her hands. "If my arms hadn't been tied to the bedposts while he raped me, I think I would have killed myself," she sobbed. "But when it was over, I couldn't bring myself to do it. I wanted to live."

Houston put his arm around her shoulder. "I believe you told us enough. There is no need to go on about it. You're safe and that is the most important thing right now." He looked at the Security man. "She's been through enough. It doesn't serve anything to let her live through her ordeal again. You have enough evidence to put that animal away for the rest of his life."

The Security man nodded. "You are right, Mr. Houston. One last question, though. Did he commit any other violent acts to your person?"

She shook her head. "If you're asking *did he beat me* I have to say *no*." She pulled her lips into the parody of a smile. "Isn't raping me violent enough?"

"It is. Thank you for your co-operation, Miss Turner. We may contact you again." He regarded her silently for a moment. "I'm sorry this happened to you. Let me assure you, the man who did this to you will not go unpunished."

"I hope so." She dried her eyes delicately with a sleeve of her blouse.

"Oh, there is one more question. It's just a routine question. We have to ask it every woman in rape cases. Did you get all your anti-fertility shots before you came to Epsilon?" He coughed into his hand. "I know it is required of every female who comes here, but sometimes..." He spread his hands. "You know, once in a while we get some woman who because of religious or other reasons doesn't believe in birth control. It happens more often than you think. It can cause some problems."

"I had all of my required shots." Tara threw a quick glance at Houston. "It's not that I thought I would need to be protected, but..." A soft blush tinted her skin.

"No need to explain, Miss Turner. That's all for now." The Security man smiled at Houston. "I assume you have transportation to get home?"

"I have. This time." He gave the Security man a sour smile. "Thank you for asking."

"No problem."

Houston took Tara's arm and led her through the maze of desks toward the exit. The guard at the front desk recognized Houston and lifted a hand in greeting. "It seems you've stirred up some kind of hornet's nest. This place is abuzz with the discovery of the Spider post underneath Epsilon City," he said. His eyes rested on Tara. "I see you've found your girlfriend."

"She is not..." Houston didn't finish the sentence. "Yes, I found her." He reached for Tara's hand. "Come, let me take you home."

She didn't pull her hand away, not even once they were outside in the corridor. His scooter wasn't parked far away and when she sat behind him, she put her arms around his chest and held on for dear life. He could feel the pressure of her soft breasts against his back and wished things were different.

"I'm tired," she said when she slid off the scooter.

He opened the door to his apartment and let her enter first, holding the door for her. He felt awkward and at a loss for words. In his mind he could see the grinning visage of Trevor Fullborne and his naked, tattooed body lying on top of Tara. His...

He raped her, the bastard. I should have killed him.

But at least she had been spared the fate the other girls suffered. To be ripped apart by a mob of ferocious hungry creatures while alive and conscious was something he could not even imagine.

"Are you hungry?" he asked.

She shook her head. "Just something to drink, if you don't mind."

"I have Fernapple juice."

"That'll be fine, whatever it is."

He went to the fridge and removed a plastic bottle. Filling a glass, he offered it to her. She took it gratefully and sipped from it. "It's good," she said, her eyes distant. "I wonder what my brother is doing right now."

"You still want to go looking for him?"

"Of course. That hasn't changed. It's my reason for coming here. You said you would help me in my search. Does the offer still stand?"

"I promised, didn't I? But I think we should wait a few days until you're back on your feet."

"Waiting will only make matters worse. The sooner we get going the better." She closed her eyes and opened them again to stare at him. "I can't get his countenance out of my mind, his forked tongue between my lips, the smell of his breath, laced with alcohol and drugs, in my face, the rings in his ears jiggling as he moved on top of me. I can still feel the pain as he forced..."

"Please, don't torture yourself by recalling what he did to you. I promise it will fade with time. Think of something pleasant."

She sighed. "I can't think of anything pleasant right now."

He sat down beside her on the small sofa and put an arm around her shoulder. "I know this will sound strange but count yourself lucky. Instead of keeping you in his apartment, he could have decided to take you into the lair of the Tunnel Rats. You might be dead now."

"Lucky?" She chuckled. "I guess I am lucky when you look at it that way." A slight shiver ran through her body. "That must have been awful. Those poor girls. How can anyone be so pitiless? I cannot even imagine that people like those Tunnel Rats exist. They should have been executed. All of them!" She spat out those last words.

"Don't worry. They will get what they deserve. That new Chief of Security strikes me as a tough guy."

"I wouldn't know. I never met him."

"I think we should go to sleep. Tomorrow you'll view the world with different eyes. We could check with Registration and see if we can find out when your brother left Epsilon City and where he went from here."

She gave him a little smile. "I don't know what I would do without you, Dave. You are such a good person. I'm glad I turned to you for help."

"I've done what every descent guy would have done. Now, get some sleep."

She yawned and got up. Before she went into the bedroom, she turned and said, "You know, I feel guilty about sleeping in your bed. Are you sure it's all right?"

He waved her on. "Don't worry about it. I'm quite comfortable on the sofa." He grinned. "This way I'm closer to the fridge if I get hungry or thirsty at night."

He watched as she closed the door to his bedroom. He wished he could hold her in his arms, cover her face with kisses and comfort her, but that would not have been appropriate. Having been raped repeatedly by a man was a burden she would carry for a long time. She may never again long for the loving embrace of another man.

He hated the man who did this to her, and he hated himself for not having been able to help her.

He went to the fridge and took out a bottle of beer, wishing he had something stronger to drink.

———

The registrar behind the counter looked up from his computer screen. "Sorry, I don't have much to tell you. Gilbert Turner left Epsilon City five years ago. He was heading for one of the mining towns up north, a place called *Lizard's Tongue*. There are no records of him ever coming back." The man shrugged his shoulders. "We have no way of keeping track of the miners or of anyone for that matter once they leave Epsilon City. It's a rough environment out there. People move from one place to another. Sometimes a new town is created, but many don't last long." He gave Houston a sideways look. "People die out there. Nobody really cares. That's the reality of it."

"He went looking for gems," Tara said. "Are there no records of him ever trying to sell anything?"

"None, Miss. Unfortunately, we don't have access to the records the Trading Commission keeps. You might be able to find something there."

"The Trading Commission doesn't give out any information. They don't have to answer to anyone," Houston said bitterly.

The registrar shrugged. "There is absolutely nothing we can do about that." He bent forward and, lowering his voice, he said, "Rumors have it that the High Commissioner has more power than the Chief of Security. Chief Moore used to ask Commissioner Quintana for advice. It's all politics, you know."

"Well, the new Chief may not play the same game," Houston said. "He strikes me as the kind of man who makes his own decisions."

The registrar laughed politely. "He won't have much of a choice. The Trading Commission runs the affairs of Epsilon."

"If you say so. I have the distinct feeling there'll be a new wind blowing soon in Epsilon City and, possibly, all of Epsilon. Anyway, thank you for your help, however small it was. At least we know Mr. Turner's first destination." Houston was somewhat disappointed about the lack of information available to ordinary citizens. He suspected Security had more in their files, but only government people would be able to get to it. He didn't even consider trying the office of the Trading Commission.

That left only one choice. They had to travel to Lizard's Tongue and see if they could trace Gilbert Turner's path from there.

Tara must have had the same thoughts, because when they were outside the registrar's office, she said, "Is there any way we could visit Lizard's Tongue?"

Houston didn't want to raise her hopes. "It won't be an easy trip, but it is possible. Let me warn you though, don't expect too much. We might be chasing a wild lizard."

She smiled at that. "I've never heard that expression before. It must be something unique to Epsilon."

"What do the Belters say?"

"We say *it's like trying to catch a rogue asteroid*."

"Well, as long as we both know what we're talking about."

She heaved a little sigh. "I have to try and find him, Dave. I didn't come all the way here to give up because of a few obstacles. I never expected it to be easy. Gil would do the same if he were the one looking for me."

"I'm sure he would. I would too if you were my sister."

Throwing him a sidelong glance, she said, "What if I weren't your sister? Would you still try everything in your power to find me?"

"Depends on what kind of a relationship we would have."

"How about lovers?"

He chuckled. "Silly question. Of course I would stop at nothing to find you, even if it would take me into the deepest jungle on Epsilon."

She touched his hand in a fleeting gesture. "It's nice to imagine someone would care that much for me."

"I care for you now, Tara, and we are almost strangers," he said gently.

Her eyes shone moist when she looked at him. "Thank you for being here, Dave."

He wanted to take her into his arms and kiss the tears away but knowing it would be the wrong thing to do, he just patted her shoulder in an awkward gesture. "We should make plans," he said, feeling as clumsy as his gesture. "I'll take leave of absence from my job. I have some holidays coming anyway."

With a happy little cry, she flung her arms around his neck. "You're the best, Dave. I promise, some day I'll make it up to you."

"You don't have to promise me anything," he said, embarrassed and uncomfortable by her soft body pressed against his. He didn't know what to do with his hands. "I'm just happy to help you."

"When do we leave?"

He laughed at her eagerness, pleased to see her smile and the light coming back into her green eyes. "Not so fast, sister. My sources told me a group of miners came to Epsilon yesterday. They'll probably leave again in a few days. Maybe we can join their group and hitch a ride with them."

"Where can we find them?"

"Probably in the Trading Commission habitat. That's where they'll be delivering their gems and whatever else they found. All deals are made there."

"Can we go there right away? I'm anxious to get going." She shook strands of red hair out of her face. "I just want to get away from this place as quickly as is possible. You know what they say...a change in location is good therapy."

"We can go there right now, if you want."

"Then let's."

The hot, humid air hit them as soon as they left the dome of Epsilon City. The sun shone brightly in the always-misty sky, but that meant little. Clouds could build up fast and bring rain. Houston squinted at the dazzling sun. The inside of the dome was not lit up this brightly and it took a while to get used to the light outside.

There were a few ships parked on the tarmac. Cranes with the symbol of the Trading Commission painted on all sides were busy loading containers from small trucks into one of the ships; goods they would take back to Earth.

Not far from them, a black warship of the Solar Union Space Navy sat on the tarmac like a giant vampire moth, ready to leap on unsuspecting prey. He remembered the big man in a camouflage uniform leaving Security Headquarters with a bunch of Union Troopers when he went to report Tara's kidnapping. Obviously, he wasn't in Epsilon City anymore, but one of his ships was.

The Security man at the desk told him Epsilon was under Marshall Law. There was something big brewing and he wondered what it was. Nothing pleasant, of that he was certain. Maybe they were at war with one of the Reptilian races. He didn't believe the Union Troopers were here because of the discovery underneath the city dome. Those Spider eggs had been there for thousands of years, apparently, and nobody, except for the Tunnel Rats, had known about them. Chief Stonewall cautioned him to keep the knowledge of what they found a secret. The fewer people knew about it the better. There was no reason to create a panic. The Military would handle it.

He shrugged mentally. He had enough immediate problems to worry about. The population of Epsilon was not large enough to be anyone's target. The presence of the Troopers was probably merely a precaution to ensure nobody decided to occupy Epsilon while the Solar Union was busy fighting a war.

The scooter rolled easily across the pavement that led to the habitat of the Trading Commission.

The bubble was huge, a small city by itself. It contained offices, living quarters, trading posts, and large warehouses. Mainly warehouses to store all of the stuff that was brought here from all over the planet. The place was a treasure house.

Before they could enter the habitat, they had to undergo a security check. Houston left his scooter on the parking lot outside the habitat, and then they walked to the checkpoint.

He handed the guard his Identity Card. The guard scanned it and gave it back to him. When he scanned Tara's Card, he said, "You've just arrived on Epsilon?"

She nodded. "A few days ago."

"What is your purpose for entering the Trading Commission habitat?"

"I want to get a permit to mine gems." She smiled at him. "I heard there is a fortune to be made on Epsilon."

The guard regarded her with a mocking grin. "Everyone comes here with dreams of leaving rich. Mostly men. I've never seen any of them leaving with riches. Epsilon is not Paradise. It is Hell. You're a woman. How much chance do you think you have?"

"I won't be alone," she said. "My friend will be with me."

The guard chuckled, looking at Houston. "I hope she's worth the trouble she will cause you, friend."

Houston smiled. "I'm touched by your concern. Just because others have not succeeded doesn't mean we won't. There is always the exception. Miss Turner is determined. Maybe she'll be the one."

"Well, good luck. Dream on." The guard smirked. "Go ahead. You're cleared. There is one thing, though. She is a Belter, not a citizen of Earth. Make sure she doesn't stray into restricted areas."

They entered the habitat though a revolving door. Beside him, Tara took a few deep breaths. "I guess I should appreciate the cool fresh air. That air outside is brutal."

"You'd better get used to it," Houston said. "Once we're away from Epsilon City, there will be little comfort. Like that guard said... Epsilon is not Paradise. It won't be a relaxing holiday out there. It's going to be tough. You still have a chance to change your mind."

She shook her head. "My mind has been made up. I'm not made from candy. Don't worry about me. I won't melt in the heat. I'm tougher than you may think."

"Okay. As long as you are sure. Once we leave here, there is no return."

She laughed softly. "You sound so ominous. Of course we'll return. With or without my brother, but we will be back. Both of us. You and me." She grabbed his hand and held on to it as if to emphasize her words. He liked holding her hand and didn't let go. They walked like two lovers out for a stroll.

The place was abuzz with transportation vehicles traveling on the wide road between the buildings; some of them leaving through the large entrance doors to take more goods to the waiting ship outside. Uniformed guards carrying flash rifles were present everywhere. They were members of the Trading Commission's Security Force.

"This place looks larger from the inside," Tara observed.

"You are right, it is big. You could spend hours exploring...if they let you. They don't like it if outsiders snoop around."

"Who lives here mostly?"

"The High Commissioner, of course, and the majority of clerks with their families. Everyone who resides in the bubble is still a citizen of the Solar Union. The men and women who work the cranes and transport vehicles are citizens of Epsilon. There is a reason for that. The majority of Earthers living here don't like to leave the safety of the habitat."

"Are Epsilon citizens not citizens of the Solar Union anymore?"

"Sure, some of them are, but you must remember that many who come here are from the colonies, from the Asteroid Belt, and other planets and from the moons in the Solar system that don't belong to the Union."

"Are there any children living in here?"

"Oh yes, quite a few. They have their own schools. You may have noticed a second habitat behind this one. That one is mainly for relaxation. It consists of a giant park with pools, grass, trees, a playground for the children, and sporting equipment for the adults."

"The Trading Commission must be very rich to have built all that."

"Yeah, from the sweat and misery of the miners and treasure hunters on Epsilon," Houston said bitterly.

"That is not really fair." Tara sounded upset. "Can the government of Epsilon not do anything about that?"

"Epsilon doesn't have a government. We're not independent. The Solar Union still owns the planet."

Tara snorted. "By Solar Union you mean Earth and the Trading Commission."

"You got it." Houston pointed down the street. "The trading posts are behind the administration buildings. We'll try our luck there."

It didn't take long before Houston spotted a group of men dressed in the khaki outfits miners preferred to wear. The dull brown-yellow blended easily with the mushroom stems and hid them from searching predators. If they were lucky.

The men seemed busy checking out tools one of the supply stores displayed.

Houston approached the nearest of the men. "Ho there. How's luck treating you these days?"

The man turned at hearing Houston's voice. "Who wants to know?"

"I'm David Houston. I've been playing with the idea to leave Epsilon City and go to one of the mining towns."

The man studied Houston for a moment. Then he screwed up his face and rubbed the stubbles on his chin. "Luck's been treating us fairly. It's the Commission that's screwing us royally. If they'd pay us a fair price for our gems, we'd be rich in a short time. As it is, we can barely afford to buy new stuff."

Houston leaned closer, lowering his voice to a conspiratorial level, "I don't know if you've heard, but there are rumors things will change. The Military have taken over Epsilon. Chief Moore has been replaced by some new guy. I've met him. He's tough, but I got the impression he's fair and won't take any shit from the Trading Commission. So I was thinking, now might be a good time to go and try my luck out there."

"Well, any change is welcome. Maybe there is hope yet. What did you have in mind to search for?"

Houston shrugged. "My wife...that's her over there studying the tools and stuff we might need." He lifted his chin to indicate Tara. "Her brother's been mining some precious stones, but we haven't heard from him for quite some time. We were planning to go to Lizard's Tongue, that's where he went, and maybe find him and join him."

"Lizard's Tongue? Hmm." The miner looked at Houston, one of his eyes squinting. "We'll be heading that way in a couple of days. Just passing through, mind you. We'll be heading further north. Lizard's Tongue is a rough town." He glanced over at Tara. "Are you planning to take her with you? I mean she doesn't look very tough."

Houston grinned. "She's tough, don't worry. It was actually her idea."

"You've been outside?" the man asked.

"You mean in the jungle?"

"Have you?"

"I've been out there." Houston suppressed the memories that rose inside him. Perhaps he was a fool to go back into that hell. What he told the miner about possible changes coming was probably nothing but wishful thinking. Deep down he knew it would take more than a new Security Chief and Marshall Law to change years of corruption and excessive control.

"There is no money to be made digging for gems," the man said. "I know some people who are dealing with...uh...private companies...you know...selling drugs. We've been contemplating changing our trade, but that is dangerous business. You never know how you get paid. They may just decide to take your merchandise and leave you with a hole burned into your skull."

"Dealing with criminals usually does not end well," Houston commented.

"You sound like you're speaking from experience."

Bits of memories flashed unbidden through his mind. *They've arrested your father last night, David. I warned him not to get involved with those men, but he wouldn't listen. He said he could make lots of money, get us out of this rat hole we're living in. Oh David, what are we going to do?*

He pushed those memories away. That was the past. It was not good to live in the past. His father died in prison, convicted of crimes he did not commit, and his mother died of a broken heart. He hated the men who had done that to his family.

"I don't have much love for criminals," he said.

The man squinted at him. "Are you a Security man?"

Houston shook his head. "No, just a guide in Epsilon. I'm introducing newcomers and visitors to the amenities Epsilon City has to offer."

"Can you recommend a good place to unwind for a couple of nights?" The miner grinned. "You know what I mean?"

"I know a couple of places. It depends on what you're looking for." He was thinking of the Serpent's Fang. People looking for the unusual, for sex and drugs, searched it out. Most men coming to Epsilon City after spending time in the jungle went there. He'd be surprised if these men were any different.

The man clapped him on the shoulder. "Well, then, maybe you can be our guide. We'll pay you for your services."

Houston saw his opportunity. "You can take us with you as part of your group when you leave, that'll be payment enough," he said.

"I'll have to talk it over with my colleagues. You're sure you want to do this? You have a cushy job, why leave it all behind? Nothing but misery and hardship waits for you. Perhaps even death."

"I'm sure I want to do this. So does my wife."

The man stared in Tara's direction. "She's a looker. You'll be challenged by men who want her." He rubbed his crotch. "It can get lonesome out there and men get crazy ideas."

"We'll take that chance. By the way, what's your name?"

The miner held out a hand. "The name's Gilles Lesage. Dr. Gilles Lesage." He grinned. "I was a gynecologist on Earth. Not a very good one, I admit. Looking at all those pussies gave me ideas and I got involved with some of my patients. I lost my license. My family couldn't live with the shame, so I decided to leave. I still like pussies. Maybe you can stir me in the right direction where I can get some." He scratched his crotch again.

"I'm sure I can help you out there, Gilles. Maybe you and your friends can help me out with my problem."

At that moment one of the other miners turned to look back. When he saw Lesage with Houston, he came over. He nodded to Houston and gave Lesage a questioning look.

"Hey, Redge. This is Houston. He wants to join us when we go back," Lesage said.

"I don't actually want to join your group," Houston said. "My wife and I want to go to Lizard's Tongue, and we are looking for someone to sponsor us. We're kinda in a hurry to get away from the city and it is not easy getting a seat on the bus going north so quickly without practically signing away your future."

"I see." The man looked Houston over. "Looking for a way to become rich?"

Houston chuckled. "We're hoping. Like everyone else who goes out."

"Well, I see no reason why you can't come with us. I'm Redge Dallas. There's five of us in the group. You already met Gilles. Those three arguing with the shopkeeper are John Lamont, he's the short, skinny fellow. The tall, lanky one is Anders Bjorklund, and the big guy with the red beard is Alex Elbenheim." He laughed good-humoredly. "Without the red beard one might mistake him for Gilles. He would hate that."

Lesage chuckled and punched Dallas on the arm. "I am five pounds heavier than Alex, and I'm much handsomer."

"With your clothes on and a breathing mask over your face." Dallas punched him back. "Go, get your stuff. We want to spend some time relaxing before we head out again."

Lesage grinned, looking at Houston. "Our new friend here promised to show us the town and stir us in the right direction. Perhaps show us places we've missed the last time we were in the city."

[6]

THE ARMORED BUS ROLLED STEADILY THROUGH THE JUNGLE OF mushrooms and tall ferns. The road it followed was nearly overgrown. It was not easy to keep a road open for long unless it was well traveled. The fast-growing mushrooms and other vegetation reclaimed its right to the land the moment it was damaged by the human intruders with their destructive machines.

Tara sat beside Houston, staring wide-eyed at the scenery moving by on the other side of the window. When a small pack of Raptors appeared in the path of the vehicle, she grasped at Houston's arm.

"Are you sure we are safe in here, Dave?" Her voice sounded skeptical.

"Quite safe. They can't see us because from the outside the glass is opaque," he assured her. "They don't know that inside this tin can are tasty snacks. It's a good thing, otherwise they might just try to use their sharp teeth as can openers." He chuckled when her fingers dug into his arm. "I'm joking. The only thing able to penetrate the material of this vehicle is a flash-cannon, and they don't have those."

"I'm glad." She smiled bravely. "Maybe I should go to sleep. You can wake me when we get there."

"That's not such a bad idea," he said.

"Now *I'm* joking," she said, laughing. "In a way this is exciting and exhilarating because it is so scary. I've never seen jungle like this before, not to mention all these prehistoric reptiles."

He smiled at her enthusiasm and didn't have the heart to tell her that so far, they had not come across the scarier reptiles...the giant carnosaurs, like the Rex. Even the armored bus could not fully protect them against one of them should the king of dinosaurs be in an angry mood and decide to attack. Or an enraged Apatosaurus might feel threatened and smash its armored tail on top of the vehicle.

"Until now, we haven't discovered another planet like Epsilon. It's quite unique. Maybe that is part of its attraction."

She leaned her head against his shoulder. "I'm glad you are here with me, Dave. Nobody told me that this planet was so wild. I would have never dared to make this journey by myself."

Neither would I, he thought. *But I'm here now and I hope things work out.*

He looked around the interior of the bus, counting the people on board. His new acquaintances, the five prospectors, were sitting in their seats in front of him, sleeping, and resting from two nights of celebrating...drinking, gambling, and fucking themselves into exhaustion. They had made this journey a few times already and for them it was just another routine trip. They felt safe inside the bus.

Altogether there were fifteen people on board, including Tara and him, plus the three drivers. Among the other eight passengers he counted three women, two older ones, and one quite young; obviously *frontier brides*. That's how the prospectors called women who came to the frontier towns for only one purpose...to either find a husband or to make money entertaining lonely prospectors. Some of them started as whores and ended up as wives. Some were killed by jealous suitors.

There were still a few empty seats. Apparently, they'd be picking up more passengers in Star City.

The lower level of the bus and the small trailer it pulled were used to transport equipment, tools, weapons, and even food. Things that could not be purchased or traded in the frontier towns. Houston had bought whatever he thought they might need to survive for a while. His acquisitions included tools for prospecting, electronic navigational equipment, weapons, and clothing. What they did not need he could always use for trading. There was no shortage of eager buyers in the frontier towns.

They were lucky to have found seats on the bus. Only through their sponsors Lesage and Dallas had they been able to procure a couple of places. The last arrival of visitors to Epsilon had included a large group of desperate treasure hunters who desired to get to Lizard's Tongue and other mining towns as quickly as possible. Tales of incredible riches to be found on Epsilon had apparently reached many eager treasure seekers on Earth and they were willing to pay a fortune to get their share. It didn't really matter. No amount of money would get them a seat on the bus because the ride to the frontier towns was paid for by the Trading Commission. Their name was on the list. It was the best they could hope for.

Houston felt sorry for them. Since they had to wait for the next bus, or the next, to take them, some of them would lose their money gambling in Epsilon City. The smarter ones might make it to the frontier towns and lose their money there. Possibly their sanity or their lives. None of them would strike it rich. The Trading Commission would see to that.

He thought of Tara and her mission. In a sense she had already discovered what she had come to find out. Everyone on Epsilon knew it. The Trading Commission controlled the flow of gems, drugs, and anything else that Epsilon had to offer.

Every transaction had to go through the Trading Commission.

The prospectors, farmers, and treasure hunters were not told the complete picture when they were lured to Epsilon with stories of unbelievable riches and promises of great fortunes to be made.

Even though the trip from Epsilon City to Lizard's Tongue was financed by the Trading Commission, Houston was not fooled by this apparent gesture of good will and generosity.

People died on Epsilon. They needed to be replaced. The more farmers harvested drug-producing plants and mushrooms, the more prospectors searched for gems, the greater the profits for the company.

He possessed one little bit of satisfaction...the company wouldn't make any money from him or Tara. He had no intentions roaming around in the jungle looking for gems, drugs, or valuable metals. If everything went well, Tara would go back home and make her report, and he would finally be able to leave this hellhole behind...courtesy of the Belter's Consortium.

If everything went well!

"How far is it again to Star City?" Tara broke into his thoughts.

"About three hundred miles."

"How long until we get there?"

"It should take around ten hours, unless something happened to the road to make it difficult for travel, or we run into other dangers that can pop up at any time." He looked at his watch. "We've been traveling for five hours."

"That means we'll be on the road for another five hours. I hope I can sit that long."

"There is a toilet in the back," he said.

"I know. I've used it once already." She smiled. "All the amenities of home."

"Enjoy them while you can. Once we get to Lizard's Tongue, things will get rougher."

She sighed and let out a deep breath. "That'll be in...how long still?"

"Three days."

"That's an awfully long trip in this sardine can."

"It won't be that bad. We'll spend tonight in Star City. Tomorrow we'll have to travel only two hundred and thirty miles to Camp Diamond, two hundred miles the next day to Heaven's Hope, and then on to Lizard's Tongue. Even though it is only about one hundred and twenty miles from Heaven's Hope to Lizard's Tongue, it is the roughest part of the trip."

"Rougher than this?"

He laughed at the way she rolled her eyes, finding her extremely attractive at that moment. "This is a piece of cake, my sweet."

She rubbed her belly. "Speaking of cake...I'm quite hungry."

He pulled his pack from under his seat and rummaged around in it. "I wouldn't want you to get skinny." He handed her a small, wrapped package. "I brought sandwiches."

She took the offered package and peeled off the plastic wrap. Biting into the sandwich, she said around a mouthful, "How about something to drink?"

"Got that too." He gave her a flask. "It's only water. We mustn't forget to refill it in Star City."

———

The original builders of the giant dome that housed Star City never finished it. Nobody knew the reason. It was much older than the dome of Epsilon City.

Wider at the base, it reached only about eight hundred feet into the sky. The top of the unfinished dome was flat, a perfect landing place for air traveling vehicles, but also a place where winged reptiles could land.

The bus arrived in Star City after dark. Instead of driving the bus into the city, the driver parked it inside a large, covered parking lot. From there the travelers went into an underground tunnel that took them into the city.

They spent the night in a hostel for travelers, also courtesy of the Trading Commission. It was nothing fancy, just a plain room with one double bed.

"I'll sleep on the floor," Houston suggested.

"You'll do no such thing," Tara said. "We'll both sleep in the bed." She smirked. "After all, we're supposed to be married."

"Only in public," he reminded her. "I apologize for announcing that without consulting you first, but I did it to protect you. If the men think you're my wife, they won't hit on you. At least that's the idea. Unfortunately, not all men will honor that."

"I appreciate the thought, but I can defend myself. I'm not a helpless little girl." She touched his cheek in a quick gesture. "Stop worrying so much about me."

"I feel responsible for you," he said. "I failed you once. I won't fail you again."

She gave him a little slap on the shoulder. "Good. Now, turn around so I can get undressed and ready for bed. I'll do the same for you."

He didn't sleep well that night, disturbed by her nearness. Staying close to the edge of the bed, he lay with his back to her, listening to her soft breathing and gentle snoring. To all outward appearances, she seemed to have no problem sleeping.

He took that as a good sign. She had a strong mind and seemed to cope well with the ordeal she had gone through. Getting raped by a man is one of the most terrifying experiences for any woman, but Tara grew up in a harsh environment. He didn't know much about life on asteroids, but enough to know that the men and women who were born into the society of Belters were different from people born on Earth. Girls did as a rule not choose their husbands. They were married off by their parents at an early age.

According to Tara, the men outnumbered women in the Belt, and it was not unusual for a young girl to marry an older man or, something not uncommon either, she'd be shared by two men.

Sometimes the men would be gone for days working the mines deep in the wormholes of the asteroids, leaving their wives and daughters alone in their habitats, without protection. Sometimes pirates would pay lonely mining outposts a visit.

Rape was nothing unusual in the Belt.

Tara had told him all about it. She was no stranger to violence and forced confinement.

Whatever she told him didn't matter. He knew she trusted him, and he would never betray that trust by taking advantage of her present vulnerability. He would protect her from others...and from himself.

———

The next day at breakfast they were told by one of the drivers that they would have to stay the day and one more night in Star City. He didn't tell them the reason.

"You can spend the day any way you like," he said. "Maybe do some exploring. There is a lot to see in Star City. Or better yet...just enjoy the last bastion of civilization. After this, things will change drastically."

"What do you suggest we do?" Tara asked.

The driver shrugged. "There are some excellent small shops and restaurants on the fifth floor. It is safe to go there." He smiled. "It is pretty much safe everywhere. Star City is not like Epsilon City."

"How do we get to the fifth floor?" Houston inquired.

"For any of you who have never been in Star City let me explain a couple of things. There isn't a main road going from the bottom all the way up, not inside the city. The only road that goes up to the top floors is on the outside of the dome, but it is used mainly as a service road. You can get from one floor to the next simply by using the stairs, but not all floors are connected that way. Also, the stairs can be a bit confusing if you don't know the city. You could easily get lost. The most convenient way is to take one of the elevators."

He looked at his watch. "We'll meet for breakfast tomorrow morning at six o'clock. Bring your luggage with you. We'll depart Star City at seven. I'd like to be in Camp Diamond before nightfall."

Houston knew why. The area near Camp Diamond was infected with *Nightrunners*, a species of giant insects. As the name applied, they roamed the jungle after dark, usually in swarms of around twenty of the nasty critters. He had encountered them only once and counted himself fortunate to have escaped with all of his limbs intact.

As large as average-sized dogs, they pounced on their victims and sheared off their appendixes with sharp, powerful mandibles. A man attacked by a swarm usually didn't survive such an encounter.

The travelers would be safe inside the bus, but the *Nightrunners* had the habit of attaching themselves to the underside of vehicles and, once the vehicle stopped, they would rush the unsuspecting travelers when they left the safety of their vehicle.

Houston and Tara left the group. They used the elevator to the fifth floor, with the intention to do a little last-minute shopping and to look around.

"You've been in Star City before?" Tara asked.

Houston shook his head. "No. I never had a reason to come here."

"It sounds like a nice place."

Houston chuckled. "Every place sounds nice until you live in it and get to know the inhabitants."

The elevator was large and filled with people. When they left the elevator, he had to admit Star City gave the impression of being nicer than Epsilon City. They entered a huge, open area that was well lit and clean looking with its tiled floor. It was ringed by small shops and eateries.

A large number of people were strolling from one place to another. Everything appeared serene and peaceful.

Tara looked around wide-eyed. "I've never seen anything like this before," she said, excitement in her voice.

"We have shopping centers like this on Earth," Houston said, "only much larger."

"I haven't been to Earth." Tara pulled him along. "Let's go into that one." Standing in front of one of the show windows, she exclaimed, "Look at all the lovely jewelry."

The storekeeper, a short, thin man, greeted them with a friendly "Hello, what can I do for you?"

"Do you mind if we look around a bit?" Tara asked.

"Of course not." The storekeeper smiled. "Everything is for sale."

"Oh, Dave, isn't this pendant beautiful? Look at these brilliant blue colors."

"That stone, my Lady, is cut from a diamond found only on Epsilon. We call it Angel Eye," the storekeeper was eager to explain. "It is quite expensive on Earth or anywhere else, but here on Epsilon..." he spread his hands, "...here it is worth very little."

"I'm surprised you are allowed to possess such a valuable piece of jewelry," Houston said.

"A good question. The Trading Commission does put limits on the pieces I can sell."

"Why would you sell it for little money if it is worth so much?"

"The price is set by the Trading Commission. I can only sell it to locals but not to visitors to Epsilon."

"I see. They don't want you to become rich, I guess. You might just decide to leave this wonderful place," Houston commented, sarcastically.

The storekeeper eyed him with suspicion. "I'm not complaining, sir. I am grateful they allow me to sell such lovely items."

Houston chuckled grimly. "You don't have to explain the Trading Commission to me, sir. The people who own it are nothing but a bunch of cutthroats and thieves."

Looking around with a haunted expression in his eyes, the storekeeper said, "I'd appreciate it if you kept your voice down and your opinion to yourself. You never know who is listening."

"I really don't care who is listening. What are they going to do to me? Shoot me for speaking my mind?"

"Are you aware we under Marshall Law, sir?"

Houston shrugged. "So I've heard. Some power-hungry Union Trooper decided to take over Epsilon, that's all I know. Perhaps it is a good thing. A change might be good for Epsilon. You may not have to worry about the Trading Commission for much longer."

"How much do you want for this pendant?" Tara interrupted the conversation of the two men.

The storekeeper let out an audible sigh, obviously happy with the change in topic. "Twenty credits, my Lady."

"Twenty credits?" Tara exclaimed.

"It is worth hundred times that on Earth."

"That much?" Tara picked up the piece of jewelry and studied it. "It is beautiful. The workmanship is exquisite. Who made it?"

"I did, my Lady," the storekeeper said proudly. "The fibrous substance surrounding the diamond is pure gold, also found in abundance on Epsilon."

Tara handed it back to him. "I love it, but I can't buy it. I am only a visitor."

"Oh. That is unfortunate." The storekeeper sounded disappointed.

"I'll buy it," Houston said, after seeing the desire and regret in Tara's eyes.

"Are you a citizen of Epsilon, sir?" The storekeeper said, hope in his voice.

Houston grimaced. "I've been here for over five years. You're considered a citizen after one year, but I suppose you know that."

"I'm aware of it. Let me wrap it up for you." The storekeeper walked to the back of the store.

Tara touched Houston's hand. "Thank you, Dave. I'll pay you back," she whispered. "I'm good for it."

"I know you are, but I don't want your money," Houston whispered back. "It's my gift to you."

She squeezed his hand. "I'll make it up to you, Dave. I promise."

The storekeeper came back and gave the little package to Tara. "Enjoy it while you are on Epsilon, my Lady, but take my advice. Don't try to smuggle it onto the ship when you leave. The punishment for smuggling is severe." He turned to Houston. "I suppose you are paying for it, sir?"

Houston pulled out his credit card. "That's what I said."

Before they left the store, the little man shook Houston's hand. "Good luck in the future," he said quietly. "I have a feeling you'll need it."

"Why would you think that?" Houston asked.

"Well, according to your credit card information, you are from Epsilon City. You are in the company of a young lady who is a visitor, not your wife, obviously, and you are on your way north to Lizard's Tongue, possibly Desert Hell."

"How would you know that?"

The little storekeeper smiled. "A bus came in from Epsilon City last night. It doesn't take much to guess the rest."

"You are a good observer," Houston said, chuckling. Leaving the store, he looked around for one of the restaurants and bars. "I'm thirsty," he said. "How about you, Tara?"

She shrugged. "Okay. I could use a drink."

———

They were on the road the next day by seven o'clock, their destination Camp Diamond.

Most of the seats on the bus were filled now. Three of the new passengers wore the official uniforms of the Trading Commission. Houston knew they were inspectors on their way to the northern trading posts of the Commission. The other eight were obviously going to the farming commune Heaven's Hope. There were two older men and two male teenagers, dressed in the black clothing of the Hottites. The two women and the three young girls wore drab, long gray dresses, their heads covered with blue hoods.

The girls were chattering away in low voices, sometimes giggling over some private joke, while the older women sat with stern expressions in their seats, throwing glances at the young girls from time to time.

The two young men kept silent in their seats, looking out of the window, watching the scenery go by.

"Does it ever change?" Tara asked suddenly.

"What?"

"The jungle outside. It gets boring after a while."

"As long as you're safe inside this bus, all those giant mushrooms may look boring, but things are far from boring should you decide to travel on foot," he answered.

"I haven't even seen any of the large dinosaurs."

"They are there, make no mistake about it. They'd make an appearance if we were a smaller object traveling through their territory. The sheer size of the bus provides us with some protection. A smaller vehicle would surely tempt them to try out their teeth and claws."

"What about those giant intelligent ants, the indigenous population of this planet?"

"You'll never see them, unless they want to be seen."

"I heard they can change their appearance."

He shook his head. "Not their physical form, but they possess certain mental abilities. They can influence your mind and make you see things that aren't there."

"Maybe that's why we haven't seen any," she said brightly.

Houston laughed softly. "Now you're beginning to understand."

"I wish I had such abilities. It would make me a super spy." She spoke with a low voice so only Houston could hear her.

"It would be a useful ability to have, but it still wouldn't help you in finding your brother," he dampened her enthusiasm.

"No, it wouldn't. Do you think we'll find him in Lizard's Tongue?"

"I can't tell you that, Tara, but it's a good place to start looking."

She reached for his hand. "I'm a little scared, you know. What if he's dead, eaten by some dinosaur? Or crippled, with an arm or a leg missing? A lot can happen in five years."

"Yes, it can." Houston was thinking of his own last five years on Epsilon. "Five years...that's a long time, but just because you haven't heard from him doesn't mean he's dead." He gave her an encouraging smile. "Maybe he found himself a good-looking frontier girl and got married. By now he probably has a couple of kids, or even three."

"Not Gil," she said, shaking her head in denial. "He's not the marrying kind."

"Many men aren't until the meet the right girl."

She glanced at him. "Are you, Dave?"

"What? The marrying kind?"

"Yes. Are you?"

He felt suddenly uncomfortable, aware of her hand still on his. "I never gave it any thought. I've been too busy trying to survive. Besides, what can I offer a woman?"

"You're a handsome man, and you are kind and caring. Those are qualities a woman finds attractive in a man," she said, looking at him.

"What about the ability to protect her from harm?"

"Sometimes circumstances are beyond our control," she said, gently, obviously guessing what he hinted at. Suddenly she laughed and leaned against him. "Did you forget that you are already married?" she whispered into his ear. "To me?"

"Just pretend-married," he whispered back.

"I know, but I love you anyway, my pretend husband." She planted a kiss on his cheek.

"It is good to see love so openly shared between a husband and his wife," a voice said beside Houston.

He looked up at the man who spoke. It was one of the two black-dressed Hottites. He held two small, wrapped packages in is hand, which he handed to Houston. "We thought you might be hungry. My wife asked me to give you these sandwiches."

Houston took the two packages. "Thank you much. That is really kind of your wife."

The man sat down in the empty seat beside Houston. "My name's Herman Reitter. My family and I are on our way to join our Brothers and Sisters in Heaven's Hope. May I ask where you're headed?"

"We're planning to try our luck searching for gems," Houston said.

Reitter made a few clucking sounds. "Have you ever done any prospecting?"

"Yes, I have."

"Then you know what you're facing. It is a hard, ugly world out there." He looked at Tara. "Especially for a young, pretty woman. Why don't you join our commune? Heavens Hope is a growing farming community."

"What do you farm?"

"Many different kinds of medicinal plants, but mainly we extract *Meskalite* from the *Devil's Horn*."

"That's a poisonous mushroom," Houston commented.

"Very poisonous. There are many different varieties. The drugs we extract have healing qualities bordering on miracles. The mushrooms grow in abundance were our community is located. We could surely use more hands to harvest them."

"It is dangerous work," Houston said.

"Not as dangerous as roaming the jungle searching for gems. If proper precautions are taken our work is quite safe. My brother Klaus and I have been doing it for over one year now. We've finally decided to bring our wives and children to the colony. We just finished building two additional protective domes. Living in our colony is as safe as living in Star-City."

Houston removed his sandwich from its wrapper and bit into it. "Thank you for the offer, but I don't believe that my wife and I would be happy living in a commune."

"Too bad," Reitter said. "You look like a nice couple." He laughed, his eyes twinkling. "You would look good in black and your wife adorable in a blue *hukka*." He held out a hand. "Well, good luck. If you should change your mind, the offer still stands. You know where you can find us."

"We'll think about it."

Reitter rose from his seat and went back to join his family.

"That doesn't sound like a bad life," Tara commented.

"Would you be happy in a commune, walking around in gray, wearing a *hukka*?"

She sniggered. "I wouldn't be seen dead wearing that on my head."

"Come to think of it, you would look cute in it," he said, grinning. "You do have that kind of face."

"Oh, you!" She slapped him on the arm.

[7]

THE BUS STOPPED AT NOON. WHEN HOUSTON LOOKED OUTSIDE, HE SAW a lake and a small habitat near the shore. It was built on a mountain of bare rock, probably part of an ancient mound built by primitive ancestors of the Uur.

"We'll take a rest period here for about an hour," one of the drivers said. "You are welcome to go outside, but don't stray too far away from the vicinity of the bus. The habitat you see is a Scouts observation post. There are no large predators in the area at this time. However, some of the smaller lizards can be just as dangerous. I suggest you take your weapons with you, just in case. Don't forget to turn on your insect repellers, but you still have to watch out for the larger insects. The repellers work only on the small, nasty ones."

He grinned. "And don't you ladies go swimming nude in the lake. It looks peaceful, but there are some mean critters in there. Some of them might even decide to take a stroll on land, so watch out." He grabbed a flash rifle and followed his companions outside.

"You want to stretch your legs?" Houston asked Tara.

"I wouldn't mind, but do you think it's safe?"

He patted the big flashgun on his hip. "This will take down most of the average-sized lizards. As far as the big boys go..." He shrugged.

"There aren't supposed to be any around. We'll take a chance. Had I known we'd make a stop in the middle of the wilderness I wouldn't have stowed away my flash rifle with our luggage.

As soon as they stepped off the bus, the hot, humid air caused Houston to gasp. It always took a moment to get used to it. Beside him, Tara did the same. He inhaled the overpowering scents of the mushroom jungle.

"Should we wear a mask?" Tara asked, still gasping.

He shook his head. "Give it a moment. Your body will adapt. There is really no danger here."

"It sure smells funny." She wrinkled her nose and sneezed. "Actually, it stinks," she said, wiping her sleeve across her nose.

He chuckled softly. "Those dinosaurs leave a lot of good fertilizer behind. Be careful not to step into it."

She threw a glance at one of the mountains of dark matter. "You can hardly miss them," she said. Houston followed her glance. The mountain of dinosaur dung seemed alive with large, shiny creatures crawling over it. He knew they were *Dung-beetles* performing their job of turning the smelly material into good soil.

They moved away from the bus. When Houston looked back, he saw the Hottite men jumping onto the soft, mossy floor, followed by the women and girls. "They don't seem to be worried," he commented.

Tara smiled up at him. "Neither am I. Not with you as my protector."

"Well, stay close to me and keep your eyes and ears open." Looking up into the sky, he saw a flock of *Draglets* sailing the air currents above the lake. Usually they would not attack Humans, not before dusk anyway, but it never hurt to be on the alert.

Huston was curious about the outpost. The habitat was not overly large, and he wondered why the Scouts would want to set up a post so far away from the more populated areas. He saw the three drivers heading in the direction of the dome, carrying their flash rifles at the ready.

"The lake looks so inviting," Tara said. "I feel like going for a swim. This heat makes my skin itchy." She scratched her shoulder. "I

94

can feel my hair matting into an unmanageable mess under my helmet. Aren't you hot?"

"Of course I'm hot, and I would like nothing better than take off my clothes and dive into that calm water, but you heard what the driver said. You may not even make it into the water before one of the denizens of the lake decides you'll make a delicious snack." He chuckled. "I wouldn't even blame them. You do look delicious when you're covered with sweat."

She poked him gently in the ribs. "You always make fun of me."

"I apologize if it offends you, but it is all meant in good spirits. I am fond of you, just so you know. I would never want to hurt you in any way...not even with words." He put an arm around her, but his eyes didn't stop roaming. Two years in the jungle had taught him never to drop his vigilance. It became part a man's being, like breathing. To do otherwise guaranteed a quick end to any quest.

She leaned into him but said nothing.

He listened to the shrill cries of *Moss-crickets* and the buzzing of the billions of *Dung-beetles* and tiny insects on the ground and in the air. A group of *Fungus-creepers* were swarming up the trunk of a nearby Mushroom-tree. Their mandibles made high-pitched rubbing sounds as they ripped out chunks from the soft bark. The noises of the smaller inhabitants of the jungle were in a way reassuring. It meant that there was no immediate danger to worry about.

"Is it like this everywhere on Epsilon?" Tara asked.

"Not everywhere. Some parts are hot deserts with nothing but blowing sand. And then there are the oceans, of course. They are rough and wild. No ships will ever sail across the giant waves stirred up by the forever-raging storms in the north. The southern parts of the oceans are much calmer, but they are not peaceful."

"I would love to go swimming in the ocean."

"Not advisable on Epsilon. The oceans are populated with giant sea-creatures. That is another reason why ships will never be able to cruise them...unless you have a ship as large as a small town."

"I've never seen an ocean. Obviously, I've never traveled on one in a ship. We have only small artificial lakes on the asteroids," Tara said with a regretful tone.

"If it makes you feel any better, I haven't taken an ocean voyage, either. I grew up in Old Chicago on Earth, in the slums. We were poor. There was no money to go anywhere. In fact, before I came to Epsilon, I've never even seen a lake, except in pictures."

"I bet you'd like to go swimming in this lake."

He shook his head, chuckling. "No, thank you. I have no such desires."

"I wonder why we've stopped here," a male voice said behind them.

Houston turned to look at the man. He recognized Gilles Lesage, the prospector he had spoken to in Epsilon City and who was essentially responsible for Tara and him being on the bus. The man squinted at the dome by the lake, one of his eyes nearly closed.

"Why do you wonder?" Houston asked.

"Because we've never stopped here before."

"Do you think there is a problem somewhere?" Tara asked, concern clearly in her eyes and voice.

"I don't want to be an alarmist, but I think there is."

One of the other prospectors joined them. He looked at Tara. "So you are the wife who so desperately wants to become rich," he said.

Tara smiled and shrugged. "I'm not the only one who is hoping to make a fortune, Mister..."

"Oh." The short man made a little bow. "John Lamont at your service, ma'am. What was your name again?"

"Tara. It's Tara."

"I hope you won't be disappointed, Tara. Do you know anything about gems?"

"A little. I'm a geologist." She smiled when she saw his eyebrows go up. "Really, I am. I probably know more about minerals and how to find them than my husband."

"That may be so, but I dare say you've never been in the jungle."

"No, I haven't, but Dave has."

"I'll make another assumption. You haven't been on Epsilon for long. Am I correct, Tara?" Lamont asked.

She threw a glance at Houston. Then she nodded and said, "Not very long."

Lamont chuckled. "I assume you two are newlyweds? Are you possibly on your honeymoon?"

"Is that so obvious?" Houston asked.

"I saw you snuggling up to each other." Lamont laughed. "I wish you luck on your search." He turned serious. "People in love sometimes forget their surroundings. Make sure you never forget yours."

"Our drivers are coming back out of the habitat," Lesage said.

They watched the three men walking toward the bus. Two other men walked with them. The two strangers carried a box between them, which they took inside the bus. Turner noticed that the two men wore Scouts uniforms.

"I knew there was something wrong," Lesage said. "That's an *Analyzer*."

"Let's hope they find whatever is wrong, because I'd hate to travel on with the scepter of a possible disaster hanging over our heads. If the bus breaks down in the middle of nowhere, we'll be in big trouble. At least here we'll be protected inside the habitat, should we be delayed," Lesage said.

The other three prospectors from the group strolled over. They had been watching the drivers also. "Looks like trouble," Bjorklund commented. He stroked his thick red beard. "If they don't find and repair the problem fast, we'll have to stay here. I don't want to be on the road when it gets dark, not around Camp Diamond. I've seen what those Nightrunners can do."

"So have I," Houston said.

"Me too," Elbenheim growled. He was the biggest man of the group. Not a man of many words. At least that was the impression Houston gained when he had shown them around in Epsilon City. The big man lifted his head and held up a hand to silence the others.

"What is it?" Lesage asked.

"Do you hear that?"

"What? I hear nothing." Lamont cocked his head, listening.

"That's it. It is too quiet," Elbenheim rumbled, looking around. "That can only mean one thing..." He let his flash rifle roll from his wide shoulder.

His companions followed his action without questioning his reason.

"What is it?" Tara whispered.

"A large visitor," Houston said, pulling his flashgun from its holster.

A scream from the group of Hottites told him enough. The scream was drowned out by a terrifying roar. Houston stared at the behemoth appearing between the mushroom trees behind the bus.

"A Rex," he said hoarsely. "And it's a big one."

Tara's fingers dug into Houston's biceps. "Look at those long teeth," she gasped.

The Tyrannosaurus swung its huge head back and forth, surveying the area. Its searching eyes fell on the group of Humans. Roaring again, it began to move. The bus was the only obstacle between it and what promised to be a feast.

Houston looked back at the habitat. Too far too run. As was the bus. There was only one thing to do, and he hoped the flash rifles of the prospectors would be powerful enough to bring down the giant lizard. He could not rely on his own gun; it was nothing but a toy against the mass of muscles and bones advancing toward them.

The Rex reached the bus and bumped it with its massive head. The bus shuddered from the impact but stayed upright. It swayed dangerously and moved sideways when the Rex smashed its head into it again but didn't topple over.

The carnosaur roared in defiance and climbed over the bus. Houston expected the roof to cave in, but to his surprise the weight of the huge lizard didn't even leave a dent.

Now the giant was in front of the bus, head tilted, and scrutinizing the pitiful Humans with small, glittering eyes, gleaming teeth in its open jaws drooling saliva. It roared and advanced slowly, leaving deep imprints in the soft ground with its powerful, clawed hind legs.

Then it stopped advancing and lifted its head, swinging it back and forth. An earsplitting roar from behind the Humans made Houston's blood freeze. He knew that sound and he knew it didn't mean good things were about to happen.

He turned his head to look at the creature crawling out of the lake.

Its head was even larger than that of the Tyrannosaurus Rex. The open maw was filled with a double row of sharp teeth, capable of ripping huge chunks of meat out of its victim. A large victim...like the Rex. A Human would mean only a tiny snack to be swallowed with one bite.

The newcomer reminded Houston of a crocodile, only many times larger. Despite its bulk, it moved swiftly away from the lake, toward the group of petrified Humans.

It seemed the only sanctuary for them had just been put out of reach.

The Rex diverted its attention away from the Humans to the new competitor for the waiting feast. The air vibrated as it let out another roar and made the decision to postpone dinner. With a speed belying its size it sauntered toward the intruder.

The giant croc roared back and met the Rex with open jaws. The Rex displayed great agility as it avoided the snapping jaws. With one mighty leap it pounced on top of the croc and tried to sink its long teeth into the croc's massive neck, but the back and neck of the amphibian were protected by thick scales, and the ripping teeth of the lizard only managed to scrape along the hard scaly surface without doing any damage.

The croc reared up, trying to dislodge its attacker.

"Don't just stand there!" a voice yelled.

Houston looked toward the bus. One of the drivers stood in the entrance, waving his arms. "This is our chance," he called out to the others. "Let's get back into the bus." He grabbed Tara's hand and pulled her with him as he ran toward the protection of the bus.

Others followed his example. They reached the bus at the same time as the Hottite family and there was a bit of confusion as they all tried to squeeze through the entrance. Even though he was as anxious as anyone to get to safety, he waited until the women were inside before he pushed Tara ahead of him into the interior. The Hottite men were close behind him.

Houston and Tara hurried to their seats to make room for the others. He saw the prospectors entering after the Hottite men, followed by the five men who had boarded the bus with him and Lesage's group in Epsilon City.

One of the drivers slammed shut the door and locked it, as if he were afraid some uninvited passenger might decide to join them.

Houston looked out of the window. The two behemoths were rolling on the ground. It was hard to determine who was winning the battle. They ripped open the ground with their clawed feet. Their tails smashed into mushroom trunks and flattened shrubs and other vegetation.

He heard Tara breathing harshly beside him. "The holograms I've seen don't nearly give you the true picture," she said, her hand on his arm, her fingers digging into his flesh. "I never would have believed animals of this size could exist and move so fast." A strange sound, almost like a sob, escaped her throat, but Houston knew it wasn't a sob.

He glanced at her. "You find this exciting, don't you?" he said.

She nodded. "As long as I'm safe in here, yes, I have to admit, it arouses me to watch such powerful creatures fighting a life-and-death battle," she whispered. "Does that shock you?"

"A little. I didn't expect it from you, but you are right, there is something exciting about this."

The two combatants had separated and were facing each other, jaws snapping. Their roars could be heard inside the bus. Even muffled they still aroused fear and terror in most of the watching Humans. Houston heard the youngest of the Hottite girls crying and clinging to her mother. The two other girls, and even the women, sat petrified in their seats, fear clearly written on their faces.

When Houston looked out of the window again, he saw the Rex had managed to get the croc on its back. The jaws of the lizard had closed on the soft throat of the croc. He could see blood seeping from the torn flesh, and it was clear that the Tyrannosaurus Rex would not loose its throne to the amphibian.

The croc stopped struggling and finally it lay still, except for the occasional twitch of the huge body. The Rex lifted its head and bellowed triumphantly, proclaiming victory over its opponent.

The king of dinosaurs proved again he was the ruler in this savage world.

The fight obviously left its mark on the mighty beast because the Rex moved a little slower as it headed back toward the place where it left the Humans. It stopped when it didn't find its intended meal. Moving the huge head slowly from side to side, it perused the empty spot. It roared once and turned to trot back to the lake.

"I believe it is giving up," Tara whispered.

"I don't think so. The Rex doesn't give up. It may have found another target." Houston squinted against the glare of the sun mirrored in the lake. "That looks like a human shape running toward the dome." Something in his awareness suddenly clicked. He looked at the three empty seats in the front of the bus. "Where are the three women who were sitting over there?"

Tara put a hand over her mouth. "Oh my god! They are still outside."

Houston jumped up and shouted, "There are three women outside. We must help them."

"If they are still out there, we can do nothing for them," one of the drivers said.

"They are by the dome. Can they get in?" He looked at the two men who had come to check out whatever was wrong with the bus.

One of them shook his head. "Not unless they have a key."

Houston stared out of the window. He couldn't see the woman he thought he had seen, but the Rex was near the lake now, searching for something.

"If nobody goes out there, at least give me a flash rifle," he said to the drivers.

"What are you going to do?"

"Help those women. I know they are out there. I've seen one of them running."

"You are out of your mind if you are trying to go against that Rex. I've never seen one this big. It'll kill you."

Houston glared at the man. "Give me your rifle and let me out!"

The man gave Houston the rifle. "It's your funeral, not mine. I'm staying in here."

101

"I'm coming with you," a voice said behind Houston.

He turned to look at Lesage.

The redheaded prospector grinned. "I've never run from a fight. I'm not starting now. Besides, I'm an expert marksman. I hardly miss my target."

"It is hard to miss one as large as that one." Houston chuckled grimly.

"I'll join you, if you don't mind," Elbenheim growled.

"In that case I'll have to come too," Bjorklund said. "You'll need someone to back you up."

All of the prospectors rose from their seats. The driver opened the door to let them out. "Good luck," he called after them.

The small group ran toward the lake, their flash rifles in front of them, ready to release the deadly bolts of energy. The Rex was moving slowly, its head down, sniffing the ground. It stopped moving and rose, lifting the narrow head, turned it to look at them.

"It spotted us," Lesage panted. "Be ready. It won't give us much time."

They slowed their run and walked toward the big beast. The pressure of the rifle's butt felt heavy against Houston's shoulder. He didn't feel at all confident. The closer they came to the giant lizard, the larger it seemed to grow.

The Rex took a few steps toward them...its jaws open in a wide grin. It stopped again when a woman shouted, "I'm over here. Please, help me."

Houston watched in horror as the woman jumped out of a thicket and began running toward them. The Rex turned and stepped into her path.

Houston fired his rifle. He knew he hit the giant lizard, but it didn't seem to slow down the charging animal.

"We're too far away," Elbenheim shouted and began running.

Another scream split the air, was cut off abruptly. The Rex lifted its head, turned back to the running men. A pair of legs was the only thing still sticking out of the open maw. Blood dripped to the ground as the Rex closed its powerful jaws. Houston shouted angrily and fired another shot into the massive body, sick to his stomach at the sight, feeling guilty for not having acted sooner.

The great lizard loomed over them, huge and intimidating, but Houston was too angry to be afraid. His heart was beating in his chest, fueled by the adrenalin being pumped into his system. All of the men were discharging their rifles. Bright bolts of pure energy sliced into the giant beast.

The Rex roared, furious at the puny creatures who dared to stand up against it, but it was clear, that it was beginning to feel the effects of the damage caused by the searing rays of heat washing over its body. Flesh began to bubble, pieces of rough skin and chunks of muscle separated and fell to the ground, sizzling like barbequed meat on a grill.

Houston concentrated on the throat, trying to remove the terrifying head from its body. One of the other men joined him in his efforts, but before they succeeded, the behemoth crashed forward, tail slashing, hind legs gauging the ground deeply. The mighty jaws snapped open and shut. Houston looked away from the grisly sight of bloody body-parts between the red-stained teeth.

"Foolish woman," Lamont said. "Had she only stayed hidden she'd be alive now."

"There were three women out here," Houston said.

Loud sobbing sounds made him look toward the thicket where the now dead woman had been hiding.

"Over there," Lesage said, heading for the thicket.

The others followed slowly, eyes alert and weapons ready.

"You're safe now," Lesage said gently into the thicket. When Houston reached him, he peered into a gap between the thorny shrubs. He saw a woman, the younger one, crouching beside a woman lying on the ground.

"Don't be afraid. It's over," Lesage said again. "We killed it."

"What about Ellora?" the young woman sobbed. "Is she safe?"

Lesage shook his head. "I'm afraid not." He held out a hand. "Come out."

Shaking her blond hair, she said, "Not without Alitia."

"Of course not. Is there a reason she is lying there?"

"She's hurt. She's can't move, but she's alive."

"What happened?"

"She got bitten by something. Suddenly she collapsed. When we saw the dinosaur, we dragged her in here, hoping someone would come to get us." She turned her tearstained face away. "I was so scared."

"You don't have to be scared anymore." Lesage squeezed his body into the narrow gap. "Come, I'll help you. Don't worry about your friend. We'll get her to safety."

He backed out of the thicket, pulling the young woman with him. She looked around with frightened eyes. When she saw the unmoving body of the Rex, she cried out, "Ellora..."

Houston pulled her against him and stroked her hair. "Don't look. It can't hurt anyone anymore."

Lesage turned to his companions. "John, you're smaller than me. Give me a hand. Someone has to crawl in there to get her out."

Lamont nodded and handed his rifle to Dallas. "Hold this for me." Then he crawled into the interior of the thicket. Lesage followed a few moments after.

"Will she be all right?" the young woman asked.

"We'll take care of her," Houston said, gently. "Let's get her back into the bus first. By the way, what's your name?"

She smiled shyly. "I'm Millie. What's yours?"

"Dave."

"Hi, Dave. I saw you with that Redhead?"

"Her name is Tara."

"She's beautiful. I wish I were that beautiful." She pulled a strand of blond hair out of her face. "Maybe then I'd get a handsome husband like you." She began sobbing again and buried her face in his chest.

Houston felt awkward and uncomfortable, holding the sobbing woman in his arms. He stroked her hair again and made soothing sounds. "You're a pretty woman. You'll find someone," he said.

Lesage and Lamont managed to carry the injured woman outside. She looked dead, but Houston noticed that her eyes were moving. Millie had said that something bit her. Obviously, some kind of poisonous reptile. There were plenty of them around.

"Let's get moving," Lesage said, urgently. "These two carcasses will attract plenty of scavengers. I don't want to come between them and their smorgasbord."

They hurried back to the bus, which seemed impossibly far away. He looked up into the sky. The *Draglets* were still cruising above. It wouldn't be long before they would come down to investigate. Millie was hanging onto his arm, afraid she might otherwise be left behind. When they got closer to the bus, he could see Tara's anxious face pressed against the window. She waved when she saw him looking at her.

From the jungle behind them a series of bellows made them increase their speed. He expelled a deep breath he hadn't been aware he was holding when the door to the bus opened. Lesage and Lamont were the first ones to enter. They carried the injured woman to the back of the bus and laid her on top of a stack of boxes.

Houston helped Millie into her seat. She gave him one last smile and mouthed the words *thank you*. He stopped for a moment to squeeze Tara's hand.

"I'm happy to see you back alive," she said. "I was so worried about you."

He saw that she'd been crying. Her cheeks were still glistening with moisture. "I'm not that easy to kill," he said, smiling, touched by her concern.

"I'm glad. But you took a terrible chance." Her eyes searched his face. "What about the woman you saw running?"

"She's dead."

"Oh, how terrible! And the one you brought in? Is she dead, too?"

"No. She's paralyzed. I'm going to find out how she's doing." When he got to the back of the bus, one of the drivers and the two men from the dome had joined Lesage and Lamont. "Can you do anything for her?" he asked.

Lesage shook his head. "Mofred believes she's been bitten by a *Rooworm*. Apparently, the ground around here is riddled with them.

105

That's why they always wear high boots and safety suits when they go outside."

One of the men from the habitat chuckled. "We don't spend much time outside. It's much safer inside."

"What about her? Can you bring her out of it?"

"She'll recover, but not immediately. She needs care and medical attention," Mofred said.

"Then you can help her?" Houston looked at Lesage. "You're a doctor. Can you do something for her?"

Lesage snorted. "I'm a gynecologist. No, correction...I *was* a gynecologist. A long time ago. Now I'm nothing but a prospector."

"Don't tell me you've forgotten everything you've learned, Lesage," Houston protested. "I'm sure there is something you can do to ease her suffering."

"How do you know she's suffering?"

"I've never seen anyone who was bitten by a Rooworm, but I've heard about it. She is in pain, believe me." Houston looked at Mofred for confirmation of his statement.

Mofred nodded slowly. "He's right. This woman is in pain."

"There is still nothing I can do," Lesage insisted. "I studied on Earth, not on Epsilon. Things here are completely different. My knowledge is useless here."

"Then what can we do?" Houston felt helpless and furious. Memories flashed unbidden through his mind. *Help me, Dave. The pain...oh...the terrible pain...I'm sorry, Steve. I can't help you...I left all the medicines back at camp...Please, Dave, there must be something you can do...The carnosaur took off my arm...my god...my arm...Dave...I'm bleeding to death...the pain...*

Steven Grant. They had been more than partners. They had been good friends. His death had shaken him and forced him to give up his search for riches. Now here he was back again, back in the jungle he had sworn never to come back to again.

He shook his head to ban the painful memories. "What can we do?" he asked again.

Mofred looked at his companion. "She'll have to stay with us. We can look after her until she recovers. What do you say, Al?"

Al shrugged. "Fine by me. I don't think Marvin and Sue will object. Sue will be happy to have someone to mother and fuss over." He gave Houston a friendly smile. "Don't worry...we'll take care of your friend."

"She isn't really a friend," Houston said. "Just another traveling companion on this bus to nowhere."

"My mistake. I just thought...never mind, she'll be in good hands."

"There is one thing, though." Houston looked down the isle of the bus until he found Millie. "She was traveling in the company of a young woman. She's sitting in the front of the bus. You should talk to her. Maybe she wants to stay behind also. She's all alone now."

"We'll do that," Mofred promised.

Houston moved back to his seat.

"How is she?" Tara asked.

"Not good, but she'll be taken care of." He leaned back and closed his eyes. The physical and mental strain of the last hour was beginning to take its toll. "I need a rest. I hope we'll get going soon. I wonder how the repairs are coming along."

"Apparently everything is all right," Tara said. "When you were outside, the driver announced that we'll leave as soon as you've resolved the problem with the dinosaur."

If it wouldn't have been such an effort, Houston would have laughed out loud.

The problem with the dinosaur! What a quaint way of putting it.

Tara's hand felt warm on his. He smiled. It was good to be back in the safety of the bus and in the company of someone who genuinely cared for him.

[8]

THINGS WENT AS SMOOTHLY AS COULD BE EXPECTED ON A JUNGLE ROAD for the rest of the journey. They reached Camp Diamond before dark. When they pulled into the parking dome, Houston breathed a sigh of relief.

He was surprised to see the size of the settlement. From the inside of the bus, it was hard to determine how many habitats made up the community, but he guessed there were more then twenty large domes strung out like a double row of pearls along the river that would eventually empty itself into Emerald Lake to the east.

A tunnel connected one dome with the next one. The parking dome was used to park vehicles and other equipment.

When they left the bus, one of the drivers directed them to the hostel in the adjacent dome. There were small shops and administration buildings in the second habitat. The residential area didn't start until the fourth one in this row. Apparently, according to the driver, the first dome in the second row was used as a recreational area, where the residents could relax and unwind without the fear of being eaten by a hungry lizard. It contained trees, grass, and even a small pond for swimming.

"People seem to live quite well here," Tara commented after hearing the driver. "Life can't be that bad."

"Don't be fooled by that," Houston warned her. "That guy works for the Trading Commission. He will paint everything rosy. I don't believe most of the people living here have the time to relax in that park. They'll be too busy searching for their imaginary fortunes deep in the jungle. Besides, living in these domes is not free. They have to pay rent to the Commission who owns all of this."

Their room in the hostel was not much different from the one in Star City. One bed for the both of them was the only piece of furniture. They had to put their things on the floor. Fortunately, their possessions were meager, and they didn't bother unpacking anything from their backpacks.

They had still a couple of hours until supper. "How about going and checking out the park?" Tara suggested.

The park was as the driver had subscribed it. There were actual terrestrial trees growing inside. Houston recognized poplars and willows. He knew they were fast growing on Earth. It seemed they grew even faster here. None of them could be older than five years. Camp Diamond had been only a collection of three or four habitats when he arrived on Epsilon five years ago. Maybe somebody had been growing the trees in another habitat.

The grass was a local variety, kept cut short by the staff that looked after the park. Benches provided places to rest and watch the people swimming in the pond. There was even a small beach of white sand at the edge of the pond.

"Oh, this is wonderful," Tara exclaimed. "Reminds me of home. I think I'll go for a swim." She looked at Houston. "How about you, Dave?"

"I have no bathing suit," he said.

She laughed gaily. "Neither have I. We'll swim naked. Look..." she pointed. "We won't be the only ones. They are nude."

Houston looked. She was right. He saw three young girls and a couple of young boys. All of them naked. One of the girls was older, possibly in her late teens. He could tell by the size of her breasts. He had no intentions joining them in the water in the buff. "No, thank you. I have to decline."

"Oh." She pouted a little. "I'm going in without you." True to her word, she stripped in front of him and put her clothes on the bench beside him. "Make sure they don't disappear," she said, laughing, "I only brought a couple of changes."

He tried not to stare at her nude body but couldn't help noticing that she looked the way he had envisioned her. Her breasts were not overly large but not small, either. They were solid, as were her round buttocks. He watched her run to the pond and dive into it, surprised at her agility and control of her body.

After swimming a few lapses, she talked to the girls in the water for a while. He could hear her laughing. She sounded happy and without a care in the world. In a way he envied her. She had no idea what waited for them. This was probably the last time she was able to enjoy an environment that was safe and clean.

When she came back, he didn't look away. She knew he was watching her, but she didn't make an effort to cover herself. He took that as a good sign, if not somewhat disturbing. Was she teasing him, or did she want to tell him something? He didn't know.

"I should have brought a towel," she said, standing in front of him, shivering a little. She used her hands to dry her skin.

Seeing her running her hands over her body didn't help at all. The pounding in his loins and the pressure of his rising member against the material of his pants reminded him of his desire and needs. *How I wish I could run my hands over your body.*

He remembered thinking the same thing the first time he saw her in the tour bus after she'd been pestering him with questions. He should have known then she'd be trouble and bring changes into his life. "Maybe you should get dressed," he said, avoiding her eyes. They seemed to mock him, but maybe that was only his imagination.

"Am I that unpleasant to look at?" she teased him.

"Not at all. To the contrary. Perhaps that is the reason you should get dressed," he said, trying to cover up his embarrassment with a little laugh.

"A husband should enjoy looking at his wife," she said with a mocking smile.

"If I were your husband I probably would do more than just enjoy looking at you," he responded. He wanted to get up, but the pounding in his loins was stronger than ever and he wouldn't be able to hide his erection.

He was certain that she was aware of the uneasiness she caused him, and he cursed her silently. This was a side of her he had not seen before, but he had to admit that he liked it. He desired her more than ever.

She dressed slowly...in front of him, as if enjoying his discomfort. He looked away, toward the pond, but seeing the naked young girls frolicking in the water didn't actually ease his anxiety, in fact it only increased it.

"I'm surprised there are not more people in the park," he said, trying to get his thoughts onto another track.

"Maybe they are all working," Tara said.

"Maybe." He looked at his watch. "I think we should go have supper. We don't want to miss it."

Supper was simple. Meat and boiled tubers, but it was nourishment and it actually tasted quite nice. After supper, they strolled down the centre street that ran through the settlement.

"This is so beautiful and peaceful here," Tara said, hanging onto his arm. "Perhaps some day we can find a place like this to live in."

Only the low ceiling of the connecting tunnels reminded Houston that they were inside an artificial habitat. It almost felt like walking down a street in a town on Earth, and he had to agree with Tara that it was a beautiful place. The houses on either side of the street were of simple and practical designs, but they conveyed a measure of security. It was difficult to imagine that on the other side of the invisible barrier ferocious giant creatures roamed a hostile, brutal world where every day was a fight for survival.

Soon they'd be entering that world. Houston hoped he could protect the enthusiastic and somewhat naïve young woman strolling by his side.

They met a number of people on the street, most of them walking, a few on scooters, similar to the ones in Epsilon City. Everyone was friendly and gave them a nod of greeting. A couple stopped and asked them if they were one of the newcomers moving into the new habitat at the end. When Houston told them that they were only passing through on their way to Lizard's Tongue, they wished them good luck.

"This is the last bastion of civilization," the man said. He threw Tara a strange look when she burst out laughing. "What is so funny about that?" he asked.

"I'm sorry, I wasn't laughing at you. It is just...our driver told us the exact same thing back in Star City. Perhaps we'll hear it again in Lizard's Tongue."

The man shook his head, his eyes solemn. "No, you won't, young woman. This is truly it. Lizard's Tongue is nothing like this, believe me."

In a way they were sorry when they had to go back to their room in the hostel. They both knew that this had probably been the last time they were able to enjoy the comforting relative safety of a civilized place.

At least, the bed was quite comfortable, and Houston looked forward to a good night's rest. He didn't feel as uneasy anymore as the first time sleeping in the same bed as Tara.

Just like an old married couple, he thought.

Sleep didn't come immediately. He saw her naked body in his mind as she came out of the pool, running toward him, her white skin glistening with moisture and her breasts taut from the cool water, nipples hard and thick.

When he finally fell asleep, his dreams were plagued by roaring dinosaurs and visions of vultures ripping into the soft flesh of dead women. He awoke bathed in sweat to discover he had slept for only a couple of hours. Tara lay breathing softly beside him, oblivious to his discomfort. He got up and went into the hallway outside, looking for the community bathroom.

As he walked down the darkened corridor, he turned when he heard the deep voice of Elbenheim.

"Can't sleep either?" the big man asked.

Houston nodded. "I can't seem to get the image of that woman being eaten alive by the Rex out of my mind," he said. "If we only could have been there earlier, we might have been able to save her. I hate this fucking planet."

Elbenheim chuckled. "I had the impression you were eager to get out there and make your fortune."

"I gave that impression, didn't I? Well, let me tell you the truth. I'm here only because of Tara. She wants to find her brother. I couldn't give a shit about all the treasures buried in the jungle or anywhere else."

"Well, well, you are bitter. I hope you find him soon, and I hope he is worth your sacrifice. You must love your wife very much."

Houston's eyes were thoughtful when he looked at the other man. "I guess I do," he said. "Why else would I do this?"

"You're a lucky man, Houston. By the way, I see you're wearing fancy pajamas, a mark of the civilized man. A few months out in the wilderness and you'll sleep with your clothes on. Or completely naked. Pajamas are nothing but useless baggage." He grinned. "What's with the pajamas anyway? You're married to a beautiful, passionate woman, man. She should keep you warm."

Houston grinned back. "I can't very well walk around naked in the corridors. What would people say?"

"You'd be surprised, my friend. Nobody really cares. Well, I hope you can sleep better for the rest of the night."

When he was back in his room, he crawled under the covers. Tara was still sleeping. He felt the heat from her body, and he wanted so much to touch her. He ached for her embrace, her passionate kisses, her love, but he knew it was only wishful thinking. She was not ready to give him her love, not after all she had been through. To take advantage of her helplessness and fear of the unknown she faced on this savage planet would be immoral and unfair.

I don't rape women. He told her that when she asked for his help, and it was still true.

Sleep came at last, but it wasn't peaceful. The nightmares kept returning. When he woke in the morning, he didn't feel rested.

Tara seemed cheerful. Yawning, she said, "I heard you get up last night."

"You did? I thought you were lost in your dream world."

"I was, actually. I dreamed I was chased by a dinosaur, but then you came with your big gun and saved me." She smiled, a faraway look on her face. "It was a beautiful dream."

"Mine were not so beautiful. They were awful and disturbing. In fact, I didn't sleep much at all."

"I'm sorry to hear that." She reached over and ran her fingers through his hair. "You were quite happy in my dream."

"I wish I could have been there."

"But you were."

"The *me* in your dream was only a figment of your imagination. I wasn't aware of what he experienced." He grimaced. "You know what I mean. What else did I do besides shooting dinosaurs? I hope nothing indecent?"

"I'm not telling." She actually blushed a little. "Besides, it was only a dream. You have nothing to apologize for." She sat up and slipped from the bed. He got a glimpse of her bare buttocks before she smoothed out her short nightgown.

It didn't help his mood.

I'm a man, damn it, with feelings and desires. I never realized how much I need a woman. How much I need you, Tara.

"Look away," she said. "I want to get dressed."

"It didn't seem to bother you yesterday in the park when you pranced around in front of me naked," he said.

"That was different. We were in public."

Well, that really makes a lot of sense.

At breakfast, they sat at the community table with the Hottite families. They all seemed to be in good spirits, laughing and talking; the girls giggling.

"Have you thought about our proposal?" Herman Reitter asked.

"About us staying at your colony?" Houston shook his head. "As tempting as it sounds, we have other plans."

"What do you say, Mrs. Houston?" Reitter looked at Tara.

"Like my husband says, we have other plans. Besides, we don't plan on settling on Epsilon anyway."

"Where are you planning to go?"

She shrugged. "There are other colonized planets. I'd prefer one not as savage as Epsilon."

"You won't find Paradise out there, if that's what you're looking for," Reitter said. "Some of our Brothers and Sisters have founded a colony on *Devil's Nest*. In fact, my wife Elise has an uncle there. They have birds so large you'd never think they could fly. Mind you, not all of them fly. And believe me...those birds are as dangerous and vicious as the Rex your husband fought yesterday. They can carry an adult away as easily as a small child. No, there is no Paradise anywhere. Not in this life." He smiled. "But that doesn't matter. That's how everything was designed. We know Paradise waits for us after we leave this plane of existence."

"Amen," both women said.

Tara reached over and put her hand on Houston's. "My husband and I will make Paradise wherever we are." She looked at Houston. "Won't we, dear?"

Houston smiled politely and nodded. "We will, dear, we will."

The two Hottite women clapped their hands together and laughed merrily. "It is so nice to see a young couple with so much love. You would fit perfectly into our commune," Elise said.

"I'm sure we would." Tara patted Houston's hand. "Who knows, in a couple of years we might even consider it, right dear?"

"I doubt it," Houston growled.

"He's a little grumpy this morning," Tara announced.

Everyone at the breakfast table thought that was funny. Their cheerful laughter didn't do much for Houston's frame of mind.

They left Camp Diamond at eight. It was only two hundred miles to Heaven's Hope, but, apparently, the road would be rougher from this point on, and the bus wouldn't be able to travel fast. The drivers expected frequent stops to clear away debris and vegetation that had grown on the road.

———

115

Houston settled into his seat and rubbed his hands on his pants. "This is the third damn time we had to clean away debris from the road," he said.

Tara gave him an encouraging smile. "Look at it this way...you'll get exercise and fresh air while we women are stuck inside this can on wheels."

"Fresh air?" Houston snorted and then he laughed when he saw her face. He knew she was only teasing him. "It's a sauna out there. I think today must be the hottest day I've ever encountered on this planet."

"Maybe it's a good thing it is so hot. For all we know it might even keep the big lizards away."

"Fat chance of that. It most likely makes them even more aggressive...if it's at all possible."

"Your husband is right," Herman Reitter said beside them.

Houston had not seen him coming down the isle. He gave the black-dressed Hottite a grateful look. "Thank you for backing me up. I think sometimes my wife doesn't believe me when I explain all the dangers out there. I don't want her to be afraid, but at the same time I want her to be aware of everything that could happen."

Reitter smiled warmly. "I still say you should stay with us. It is much safer in our commune."

"Well, thanks again for the offer, but we haven't changed our mind. Is this part of the road always this bad?"

"Most of the time." Reitter looked out of the window. "It has to do with the wind. It seems there is a bit of a wind tunnel in this area, and it knocks down trees and other vegetation. Sometimes the road gets flooded from the rain and then we really have fun. Maybe some day we can get an airbus traveling between the settlements. It would be faster and safer."

"What about the flying reptiles? I understand that they are a problem with vessels in the air?" Houston wondered.

Reitter chuckled. "Most of that information is blown out of proportion. Sure, the Dactyls like to attack anything that invades their territory, but an airbus would be large enough to deter them."

"Then why are they still using ground buses?"

"Politics. Money. Who knows?" He patted Houston on the shoulder. "We'll be in Heaven's Hope soon. Why don't you and the wife spend the evening with us in our commune instead of in the hostel?"

Houston looked at Tara. "What do you think, sweetheart?"

"Oh, I think it would be fun, my dear husband." Tara laughed happily. "Maybe we'll like it so much there we won't leave."

"There you see," Reitter said. "You wife is already half convinced." He winked at Tara. "Well, I'd better join my family. They are anxious to get to their new home. And I am anxious to sleep in my own bed tonight. It's been a lonely year without my wife and children."

He walked back to his seat. In a way Houston envied the man. He seemed happy with his life, even though Houston doubted it was an easy one. Nothing on Epsilon was ever easy, but Reitter had his family with him, his Brothers and Sisters in the commune, and his faith. Houston had neither. He was not a religious man, never had been. Some people accepted their fate, viewing every tragedy as a test by their god. The harder their life, the more religious they seemed to become.

Houston's mother had been a good Catholic, going to church almost every Sunday. When his father went to jail, she had only her faith to keep her going.

If you don't go to church you will end up like your father, David. People who don't go to church go to Hell.

He almost laughed out loud.

Hell!

Perhaps his mother had been right. Hell was just another word for *Epsilon*.

[9]

THE BUS ROLLED ON, SLOWING DOWN ONCE IN A WHILE TO CRAWL around or over a pile of knocked down vegetation. The next bus coming back the road might have to stop and remove it unless it decayed and helped to raise the road a little.

They reached Heaven's Hope in the early afternoon. This time the driver parked the bus outside the only habitat. The Hottite families removed all of their belongings from the bus and from the trailer and piled them up beside the bus. Even before they were finished unloading, a couple of smaller vehicles pulling trailers came out of a side road. They stopped and two men in black outfits climbed out to greet the Reitters.

Herman Reitter came over to Houston. "If you'd like to take advantage of our invitation, we have room for you in one of the rovers."

"We'll gladly come with you," Tara said.

"I'll have to clear that with the drivers," Houston said. "They may not like it if we stray away from the group."

"Go ahead."

Houston approached one of the drivers and asked, "Would it be all right if my wife and I go with the Reitters?"

The driver shrugged. "Fine by me as long as you are here in the morning. We'll leave at seven sharp, with or without you."

"We'll be here." Houston shouldered his pack and walked back to the Hottites. "We accept your invitation."

"Great. Now if you could lend us a hand getting all this stuff onto the trailers, I'd appreciate it."

After the trailers were loaded, everybody climbed into the rovers. Houston rode with the men, while Tara ended up in the rover with the women. They drove down a narrow road, which was much rougher than the main road the bus had been traveling.

"This is the dangerous part of the journey," Reitter explained. "I wish we'd have a couple of armored vehicles. We are too vulnerable in these. We've been lucky so far, because for some reason there are not too many of the larger carnosaurs roaming this area, and we can deal with the Raptors."

"It's not luck," the driver said. "It's the Good Lord watching over us."

"Amen, Brother. Amen." Reitter said.

Houston watched the jungle outside, a bit uneasy and not feeling secure at all. Should they encounter a Rex or any of the giant dinosaurs there would be no safety inside the rover.

"We do have a small flash-cannon mounted on top of the roof," their driver said. "It is not quite as bad as Herman makes it sound. It'll knock down even a Rex if we hit it in the right spot." He chuckled. "Sometimes you have to give the Good Lord a hand."

After traveling for about half an hour, the road ended in front of a tall gate, which was part of a cross-link fence. Inside the fenced-in area Houston saw a number of habitats. He also noticed the absence of tall mushroom trees.

"Welcome to Heaven's Hope," Reitter said. "Our community is protected by an electric fence. It keeps away even the largest carnosaur. The only danger threatening us comes from the air, but we have even that under control. Most of the time, anyway. There is no complete safety anywhere on Epsilon."

The gate swung open, and the two rovers entered the fenced-in community. The road inside was smooth and better maintained. To his surprise, Houston saw sheep and goats inside a corral without a protective roof above them. He pointed at the animals. "Aren't you afraid winged predators might take them from the air?"

"We have a robotic controlled weapons system that has worked quite well so far. The Dactyls are actually pretty smart. They have learned to stay away from our community." He chuckled. "They know they are not welcome here."

"As you can see, we live without fear, protected not only by the habitats but also by an electric fence that allows us to walk around outside," Klaus Reitter, who had been silent most of the time, added to his brother's words.

"But you still carry rifles, even inside the fenced-in area," Houston remarked when he saw a few people walking on the road, rifles slung across their backs.

"Just an extra precaution. As I mentioned before, Epsilon is not a world where you can ever feel completely safe," Herman Reitter said.

His brother chuckled. "We put our fate into the hands of the Good Lord but, as Jeremy already said, it doesn't hurt to have some additional insurance."

"Amen," Klaus Reitter and the driver said.

They drove to the end of the road and halted in front of the last two habitats. The rover with the women stopped beside them. Houston and the other men climbed out and waited for the women to get out of their vehicle.

"Our home is in this habitat," Herman Reitter said to the women. They clapped their hands and laughed happily.

"Everything is beautiful," his wife Elise exclaimed. She came over to the group of men and hugged her husband. "I think we'll be happy here. It's just like you told us."

"There are sheep and goats over there," one of the girls said with an excited voice. "Can we go and have a look at them?"

"Maybe later," Klaus said. He looked into the sky and scanned it. "There are a few safety precautions we have to go over first. This is not Star City, remember that whenever you are outside the habitat. Please, go inside."

The girl made a face, clearly not happy, but she obeyed.

Tara joined Houston. "It is nice here," she said. "I like the open concept. It gives you a wonderful feeling of freedom." Taking a deep breath, she added, "It would be nicer if the air weren't so hot and humid." She wrinkled her nose. "What is that funny smell?"

"Oh that," Herman Reitter said. "You get used to it after a while. It comes from the sulfur geysers, but you only smell it when the wind blows from the east."

"I don't like that smell, it stinks," the youngest of the girls said. "It makes me want to throw up."

"Don't use such words," her mother chided her. "Go with your sisters."

The girl followed the other two with obvious reluctance. Her mother shook her head. "Young girls can be so difficult sometimes, especially that one. She was supposed to be a boy but..." She lifted her face toward the sky, "The Good Lord saw it differently. We don't always get what we wish for. I guess it is His way of testing us."

Elise patted her arm. "Now, don't start that again, Milia. We have two boys, and they were no angles when they were Cilia's age, but they turned out all right. Give her time." She looked at Tara. "I suppose you don't have any children yet?"

Tara's laugh was amused. "Thank goodness, no." She threw a glance at Houston and gave him a little smile. "Besides, we haven't been married long enough and I'm not so sure Dave wants children."

"Oh, you have to have children. Without children you are not a real family. The more children you have the greater you're blessed. The Good Lord has designed us that way." Milia clasped her hands together as if she were about to pray. "I would have been so lonely this past year without my girls, and I give thanks every day to Him for the blessing I've received."

"Yeah, well, we'll see how things develop." Tara squeezed Houston's hand. "Everything is up to Dave."

"If you ladies are finished chatting, maybe we can start unloading the rovers," one of the drivers said, obviously getting a bit impatient.

Houston, feeling uncomfortable still holding Tara's hand, moved forward. "I'll help you, of course."

"We appreciate it," Herman Reitter said. He looked up into the sky again. "It looks like we might get some rain. I want to have everything inside the habitat before that happens."

The women went ahead of them into the habitat and the men began unloading the boxes and small crates from the trailers. Some of them were quite heavy and required two men to carry them. "We bought a bunch of equipment in Star City. Most of it belongs to the commune, of course, along with the medicines and first aid kits. Mishaps occur constantly, especially with the children. It is important we have enough medicines to treat them."

As usual, the habitat appeared larger inside than from the outside. It contained four modest homes. The other three were already occupied. The homes were nothing but rectangular boxes with a flat roof. It was not necessary to make them watertight because it never rained inside the habitats. Each home was large enough to house two families with up to four children each. The children slept in one room, in bunk beds.

The women were delighted with all the space, and even Tara expressed her envy when they viewed the Master bedroom. "I think I could be happy in here. Couldn't you, Dave?"

"It seems all right," Houston muttered. He had to admit that living with the Hottites may not be as bad as he envisioned. People residing in small communities cared and looked out for each other, unlike in large cities where most people hardly even knew their neighbors, never mind worry about them.

Even the little girl looked happy. "It smells nice in here," she said to her mother.

"I'm glad you approve, child," Milia said. "Perhaps next time you don't run your mouth off so quickly. This is our new home, which the Good Lord provided for us. We must be grateful."

"I thought Daddy and the other men built this house," Cilia said, screwing up her face.

"They may have built this house, but *He* made it possible. Don't always analyze everything," her mother chided, shaking her head. "I can see trouble ahead with you."

"She's fine," Klaus Reitter said. "Give her time to adjust. We all have to adjust. I'm just so happy to have you all with me."

"Amen," Herman Reitter said. He looked at his watch. "I suggest we go to the community-dining hall. We don't want to be late. Today we are guests of the commune, but tomorrow all of us will have to start pulling our weight. You two women will have to help with the kitchen chores and you girls will start schooling." He turned to Houston. "You, of course, are our guests." He smiled and winked. "You've earned your food by helping us with the goods we brought."

The community-dining hall was in the first habitat by the gate. Most of the residents of Heaven's Hope were already sitting at the tables. Houston was surprised to see so many. He also noticed quite a few children.

There was a long table set up at one end. It was covered with pots and plates heaped with steaming food.

"We help ourselves here," Herman Reitter explained. "And don't be shy. There is plenty."

Houston waited until the two Reitter families were lined up before he and Tara went to get their food. One of the women standing by the table handed them plates. She smiled at them and said, "The Good Lord has provided us with much tonight."

"I thank you for your kindness," Houston said, hoping it was the right thing to say.

"I am only the Lord's servant. Give thanks to *Him* for the food you are given."

"We will," Tara said.

Houston and Tara received many curious stares. Everybody seemed friendly and smiled politely when he looked their way. Even the Reitter women and children were studied, and he remembered that they were strangers here also.

After everyone had eaten, Herman Reitter rose from his seat and walked over to a small podium. "May I have everyone's attention, please?" He waited for a moment to give the people time to focus on him. "As many of you know, my brother Klaus and I went to Star City a few days ago to get our families. Well, they are here now. I would appreciate it if you all welcome our wives and children to our community." He looked at his wife. "Please, stand up so people can see you all."

Everyone applauded and shouted happily when the two women, the three girls, and the two boys stood up.

Elise wiped her eyes with her hand, clearly overcome by emotion. Houston could not blame her. He felt a little overwhelmed himself witnessing the enthusiasm and outpouring of affection as the people clapped and stomped their feet. Some of them even started singing.

Hermann Reitter lifted his hand. "Brothers and Sisters, I would like you all to join me in a prayer to give thanks to the Good Lord for making this happen."

The people bowed their heads while Reitter prayed.

When he was finished, they shouted, "Amen."

Houston turned to look at Tara as her hand stole into his and saw tears in her eyes. "This is just so wonderful, Dave," she whispered, dabbing at her eyes. "So much love."

He put his arm around her shoulder and held her close for a moment.

"This could be yours also," Milia said to them, her face glowing with happiness. "You should forget about going back out there and stay with us. You'd be welcome."

Houston shook his head. "We'll have to find Tara's brother."

"Come back here after you found him."

"We'll see." Houston smiled politely. The offer was tempting, but he knew this life would not be for him. He wasn't sure about Tara's feelings. Everything looked always so wonderful at first, but he had no doubts that somewhere in this little paradise lurked a snake in the grass. Nothing was ever as it seemed.

Another man joined Herman Reitter at the podium. He held up a hand to quiet down everyone. "This is indeed a momentous day, my Brothers and Sisters. Herman and his brother Klaus have proved to be a valuable asset to our community, and we know that their wives and children will bring the same with them. In honor of their arrival, we will suspend all chores for tonight and celebrate."

Everyone cheered.

Women came out of another room in the back, carrying bottles and cups. They put them on the tables.

Herman Reitter joined them at their table and clapped Houston on the shoulder. "Celebrate with us, my friends. Tonight, we drink wine and give thanks for our blessings."

It didn't take long before everyone was in a happy mood. People sang and danced. Houston noticed that Tara drank more than she should be doing and seemed to be getting giddier as the evening progressed. She giggled a lot and leaned against him, touching his hands and face.

Normally it wouldn't have bothered him, he might even have enjoyed her attention, but he felt a bit embarrassed by her too obvious show of affection in public. "You're overdoing this happily-married bit a little," he whispered into her ear. "No need to go overboard."

She just laughed and whispered back "Who says I'm going overboard? I'm showing my love for you, that's all."

"That's good," he mumbled, "Just don't overdo it."

"Come, dance with me," she said.

"I've never danced in my life."

"Then you don't know what you're missing, Dave. Dancing is an expression of happiness. Come on, I'll show you." She dragged him to his feet.

"Go on, dance with your wife," Elise urged him on, laughing, her voice slurred. It seemed to Houston that she also was emptying her cup much too often. It occurred to him that it was highly unusual for religious people to drink so much wine. In his experience, religious groups usually didn't allow any consumption of alcohol.

Shrugging, he followed Tara reluctantly with the knowledge that he would make a fool of himself.

I've got two left feet when it comes do dancing, damn it.

But nobody seemed to notice him shuffling around on the dance floor. Tara pressed her body against him and sang along with the music. He hadn't even been aware of the two women by the podium playing some kind of string-instrument and the man who played a small accordion. He recognized the vertical keyboard because his father had played an old, battered version of it.

Tara stroked his neck with warm fingers as they danced to the music. It felt nice, but he was happy when they finally went back to their seats. Wiping the perspiration from his forehead, he stared into his cup, tempted to take a deep swig, but he drank only a little. He didn't feel like waking up in the morning with a hangover and a headache.

It was quite late when the celebration ended.

"I think you'd better stay overnight," Herman Reitter told them. "It is too dangerous to travel through the jungle at this time of night. We'll get you to your bus in time tomorrow morning."

Back in the new home of the Reitters, Milia made up a bed for them in the living room. Elise excused herself with a little giggle. "I think I drank too much of the juice," she said.

When everyone was gone, Tara undressed and, naked, she slipped under the covers.

Houston rummaged around in his pack for his pajamas. "Aren't you going to wear your nightgown?" he asked.

She giggled. "I'm much too hot for that. I think you should sleep naked too."

"I don't think so." He undressed and put on his pajamas. When he joined her under the covers, she immediately snuggled against him. "Aren't you tired?" he asked, unable to control his body reacting to her nearness. He could feel the heat of her body.

She kissed him and began to unbutton his pajama top.

"What are you doing?" he asked, feeling uneasy by her aggressive behavior.

"What do you think?" Her hand stroked his chest and slowly moved across his belly. With a loud sigh, she reached into his pajama bottom and curled her fingers around his erection.

He groaned, surprised by this unexpected action. Pushing her away, he said, "Control yourself, Tara. You are drunk."

He felt her go rigid then turn away from him.

When he heard her sob, he wanted to put his arm around her but refrained from doing so. He hated what he had done, but he could not take advantage of the situation. She was not herself. Had he given in to her obvious invitation it would have been like raping her. She'd thank him in the morning.

He slept uneasy, turning many times. When morning came, he

didn't feel rested. He rose before Tara did and got dressed. Then he used the washroom to wash up. After that he waited for everyone to wake up. It was still dark outside, and when he checked his watch, he discovered it was shortly after five. If they wanted to catch the bus, they had to leave in about an hour.

Sitting on the chesterfield, he heard Tara moving. She sat up and looked around. When she saw him, her lips began to smile, but then her face suddenly hardened, and she looked away. Pulling the covers around her, she went to look for her clothing and dressed in silence.

She didn't look at him when she went into the washroom.

Houston sighed, wishing he could erase what happened the night before. He had done nothing wrong, except refuse her, but he felt guilty about something.

Damn it! Women! It didn't matter what you do, it is never the right thing. They always make you feel guilty.

"Good morning."

He turned to smile at Elise, who stood in the hallway, stretching. She seemed in good spirits, despite the wine she had consumed. "Did you and Tara sleep well?" she asked, yawning.

"As well as can be expected," he answered.

"Where is she?"

"In the bathroom. She should be finished soon."

Elise put her hand against her head. "I have a bit of a headache." She gave a little laugh. "Too much wine. I noticed Tara likes her wine, but you hardly touched any."

"Was it that obvious?"

"To me it was. But that's okay. Herman doesn't drink at all. He doesn't mind if I do, though." She laughed again, almost embarrassed. "It relaxes me and makes me..." She fluttered her hand, color creeping into her cheeks. "You know what I'm talking about. I mean...Tara...you know...the alcohol seems to affect her the same way."

"I guess it does." He felt uncomfortable with the subject. He wasn't used to discuss personal things like that with a woman, especially a woman he hardly knew. It surprised him anyway that Elise

127

seemed so forward, since in his mind he had labeled her as overly religious and quite uptight.

At that moment Tara came out of the bathroom. When she saw Elise, she smiled and said, "Good morning."

"Good morning to you also. How is your head?"

Tara forced a laugh. "Probably as clear as yours."

"That bad? Don't worry, it'll pass." She looked at her wrist. "Oh my, it is getting late. I'll better wake up Herman. He has to take you to the bus."

Tara barely looked at Houston when she picked up her pack. He didn't know what to say to her, feeling awkward with the silence between them. "Are you okay?" he finally asked.

"I'm fine. Don't worry about me." Her answer was curt and without any emotion.

"I'm glad to hear that. I mean...I'm glad you're fine, and I do worry about you."

"You don't have to. Nobody ever worried about me before, and I made it this far. I can get along just fine by myself."

"Good. I'm happy to hear that."

Hell! He didn't need this shit. If she wanted to play the game that way it was fine by him. He wasn't going to crawl on his knees and ask her to forgive him for something he didn't do. It was she who was mad at him, not the other way around.

Herman Reitter came out of the bedroom and, after washing up, he said, "Since you seem to have made up your mind about not staying with us, we'd better get a move on. If you're ready we can leave."

"We're ready," Houston said. He held out his hand toward Elise when she came to say goodbye, but she put her arms around him and gave him a hug. "May the Good Lord bless you and may you find happiness wherever *He* leads you." Then she planted a quick kiss on his cheek.

Touched by her affection, he said, "Thank you, Elise. You all have been so kind. I hope you will be happy here, also. Say goodbye to your children and to Klaus and his family from us. We will remember you all with fondness."

The trip back to the bus terminal didn't take long. It had rained a little during the night, but it didn't affect the condition of the road. They traveled in silence. Even Reitter seemed a bit depressed, as if sensing the tension between Houston and Tara.

The men shook hands and Reitter pulled Houston close, clapping him on his shoulders. "Take care, my friend. Think about what I said. You and your wife will always be welcome here."

Once they sat inside the bus, Houston realized they hadn't even had breakfast.

"We should have gotten something to eat at the terminal," he said to Tara, trying to break the icy silence between them.

"I'm not hungry," she said tonelessly. She got up suddenly and walked to the front of the bus and took the empty seat beside Lesage.

The big prospector seemed to listen to her for a while. He turned his head and looked back at Houston.

Houston heard Tara laughing, much louder than necessary. Lesage echoed her laugh and put an arm around her shoulder.

Houston closed his eyes.

Damn her! What the hell did he care what she did. They were not married. There was no commitment between them. The only reason they had acted like a married couple was to protect her. It seemed she didn't care about that anymore. Why should he?

[10]

LIZARD'S TONGUE WAS DIFFERENT FROM OTHER MINING TOWNS. THE office of the Trading Commission was situated inside a large habitat. There were also a few smaller habitats containing workshops and stores, but the majority of people lived in caves inside a mountain.

The mountain was actually a leftover mound built by primitive ants thousands of years ago. In fact, the residence called it *The Mound*. It was not as sophisticated as Epsilon City or Star City, but it was a safe place to live in. The settlement didn't have a mayor or any other bureaucrat running the place. It didn't have a jail or an effective police force. The only authority was the office of the Trading Commission, and the people working there couldn't care less about the welfare of the residents.

The bus arrived in Lizard's Tongue shortly before noon. Even though it was only one hundred fifty miles to Desert Hell, the bus wouldn't travel on until the next day. Much of the stuff in the trailer had to be unloaded in Lizard's Tongue and it would take a few hours to get it all transported into the warehouse inside the Trading Commission habitat.

Tara came back to pick up her things and went back to the five prospectors. She didn't even look at Houston.

Before he left the bus, he went to talk to the drivers. "Listen, I won't be unloading my stuff until tonight, because I might be traveling on to Desert Hell if I don't find the information I seek here. I hope that's okay?"

"Sure, just make certain you get it off before we leave tomorrow morning, otherwise it'll end up in Desert Hell without you. We'll be emptying the bus there. We take nothing back with us except gems and things like that."

He shouldered his pack and climbed out of the bus, carrying his flash rifle in his hand. Lizard's tongue was not as safe as Heaven's Hope. As far as he knew it didn't have a Security system surveying the sky in case flying reptiles decides to drop in for a visit. Neither was it safe between the habitats. The only protection one had was a flash rifle.

Since Tara decided to seek the company of the prospectors, Houston didn't really have a purpose for his visit, but he made up his mind not to let it be a reason to waste his time. He might as well go and make inquiries. His immediate destination was the office of the Trading Commission.

The office building was the first one in the habitat. The other buildings were warehouses and a small building where the employees of the Commission lived.

He stopped short when he saw the woman behind the desk. The resemblance to Tara was uncanny. Older and more mature but just as beautiful. She gave him a searching look. "Can I help you?"

He smiled and said, "I hope so. I came a long way to find someone. How are your records?"

"My records?"

"Yeah. Do you have a record of everyone who comes to Lizard's Tongue?"

"Hardly. There is no law that requires anyone who comes here to register."

"But you must have records of people who trade with you."

She nodded. "That we do, but we don't know if the names they give us are their real names. You know, the men and women who come up here are...not all of them are upstanding citizens. Some come here to disappear, not found."

"I see. I'm looking for a man by the name of Gilbert Turner. From records I checked in Epsilon City he came up here about five years ago."

"Five years? That is like an eternity on Epsilon. I doubt if there are any records of your friend." She squinted at him. "I assume he is your friend."

"No, he isn't, but his sister is."

"Where is his sister?"

"She's with some friends."

The woman shook her head. "Sounds complicated already. Let me have a look on my computer. It shouldn't take long to track him down if his name is registered anywhere." While she waited for information to pop up, she said, "I shouldn't really give out any information to you unless you are an employee of the Trading Commission, but you seem like a nice guy, and I'll make an exception."

"I really appreciate that. Let me ask you something. How did a good-looking woman like you end up here in this forsaken place?"

She laughed. "That sounds almost like a come-on, and to be honest, you're not the first one to use that archaic line, but thank you for the compliment. It's a long story. I wouldn't want to bore you. Ah, here is the information, and I'm afraid it's not much. A Gilbert Turner bought some supplies over four and a half years ago. That is the only entry I have. Sorry."

She shook strands of red hair out of her face and looked at him with her green eyes. "I couldn't help but notice you studying me. In fact, when you walked in here your jaw nearly dropped when you saw me." She winked. "Did I make such an impression on you?"

"You look like someone I know."

"A lover?"

He hesitated. "No, not a lover, just someone I might have let down. At least that's how she feels."

"A woman you love. I can hear it in your voice. She jilted you and now you feel guilty. You need someone to take your mind away from her." She glanced at her watch. "How do you feel about joining me for lunch? We have only one place here where you can eat, but they actually serve quite descent food. What do you say?"

He wasn't sure if he should accept her invitation. What if Tara saw him? What would she think?

To Hell with Tara. She's the one who left me. I don't owe her a thing.

"Sure, why not?"

"Good." She turned around and called to the man behind another counter, "Heller, I'm going out for lunch. I don't know when I'll be back."

"Okay. I think I can manage registering the stuff that's come in. All by myself. Don't worry about me. It's not that much work."

"He doesn't sound so happy," Houston said.

The woman laughed. "Now you understand why I need to get out of here for a while? That man is never in a good mood. He needs to get laid."

Houston was a bit shocked by her frankness. "So...why doesn't he?"

"Don't look at me. I might be willing, but unfortunately, he likes men better than women." She came around the counter. "Do I shock you?" She chuckled. "Don't deny it. I can see it in your eyes. But don't worry, I won't rape you." She poked him in the ribs. "Even though some men might like that."

"Some might," he said, trying to make light of her words. "But if they like it then it's not really rape, is it?"

"I guess not." Her eyes sparkled with mischief. "I like you. You can leave your stuff here," she suggested. "It will be safe. Nobody will touch it."

She waited until he put his backpack behind the counter and came back. Hooking her arm into his, she said, "You're a handsome young man. How come you're alone?"

"I could ask you the same question."

"I told you it's a long story. I'm sure you've heard a similar one before. By the way, my name is Claire Chanas. What's yours?"

"David Houston. Call me Dave."

"I will, Dave. Nice to make your acquaintance."

They left the habitat and stepped into the open. Clair scanned the sky and the surrounding area. "I didn't bring a weapon since you got your flash rifle. I hope you are good with that rifle."

"I've had some practice. Do you have problems with large predators coming into town?"

"Not so much with the real large ones, like the Rex and its cousins, but the Raptors sometimes decide to pay us a visit. They are the ones to worry about. They're cunning and smart."

"How about the Dactyls?"

"Those too. A few we can handle, but when they come in flocks, watch out. We do have a small tank with a canon, but that canon is no good against the Dactyls. We have to rely on our flash rifles." She shrugged. "That's life on Epsilon. You're safe inside the habitats but outside you're on your own. I sometimes wonder how the prospectors and miners survive in the jungle. You wouldn't find me out there."

"Only desperate people or complete fools go alone into the jungle."

"You've done it?"

He nodded. "Yes, but I learned my lesson the hard way. I lost a good friend to one of those giant lizards."

"What have you been doing lately?"

"I'm a guide in Epsilon City." He grinned. "It's much safer in there."

"But not that exciting. Am I right?"

"Maybe."

They reached the second habitat. He heard the woman beside him let out a sigh when they stepped through the entrance into the safety of the bubble. "I'm always happy to be inside. I'm not much of an adventurer."

She pulled him toward one of the buildings on the other side of the narrow street. Most of the buildings housed small stores and shops. One sign read *The Singing Barber*, another one *The Happy Taylor*. Houston smiled when he read one that said *The Grumpy Technician*.

The place they headed for was called *The Gourmet Bar and Grill*.

It didn't look any different from any eatery Houston had been to. A counter with barstools, a few tables, and a number of booths with benches. Many of the booths were filled but they managed to find one unoccupied.

The waitress came almost immediately. She was an older woman. Her face was lined, and she looked fatigued. Nodding to Claire, she asked, "What can I bring you, Claire?"

"Hi, Mildred. This is Dave. He just got here, so treat him right. Bring us your special, okay."

"Special it is. I hope you'll like it." Her tired old eyes looked at him without much interest.

"What is the special?"

"Grilled Raptor balls with steamed mushrooms. You want a beer with that?"

"Sure." Houston looked at Claire. "You?"

She shook her head. "A glass of wine."

Houston watched the old waitress walking away and wondered why she hung around in this place. Probably the same reason Claire was here. "Who runs this place?" he asked.

"Mildred runs it now, because the previous owner was eaten by a lizard." She gave a little chuckle. "Ironic, isn't it. A man who prided himself serving the best dinosaur steak on Epsilon gets eaten by a dinosaur. There has to be some justice in that. If gods actually exist, they must have been laughing their heads off."

"Yeah, that is very funny," Houston said. "I assume you don't believe in any gods?"

"Oh, I do believe in gods, but I think they give a crap about us. Look around you. Does this look like someone cares about us Humans? Not here on Epsilon. Perhaps on Earth where our gods were created, but I doubt even that. If you know your history, then you know that the majority of Humans has always lived in misery. If people didn't die of starvation, diseases, natural disasters, or accidents, they murdered each other. Here we are eaten by giant lizards. Where do you find a loving god in all of this?"

"I can't argue with you there," Houston agreed.

"I'm glad, because I hate arguing with people." Her hand reached across the table and touched his. "I believe that we have to make the best of a situation and take whatever fate gives us." A lock of red hair had fallen forward and covered half of her face and one eye. She reached up with her other hand to push it back behind her ear. He noticed a small, golden cross with a diamond inside a circle at the bottom of the cross dangling from her earlobe.

"You used to be religious," he stated.

"Why do you say that?"

"You are wearing a cross in your ear. My mother used to wear one similar to that, except for the diamond. My father was a poor man." He smiled. "Just like his son."

"You should know that a diamond is worth nothing here." She nodded. "Yes, if you must know, I used to be religious. In fact, my husband was a preacher."

"That is surprising. What happened to him?"

"He's dead. A crazy miner killed him in a rage when my husband didn't want to give him absolution after the man murdered his wife. That is how a devoted religious man gets rewarded. Now do you see why I am so cynical?"

"I can see," Houston said. "Why did the man murder his wife?"

"She cheated on him. There is no law up here. People take the law into their own hands." She moved her hand away from his. Covering her face with both hands, she let out a loud sigh. "You don't know how I hate this place."

"Why not leave?"

"And go where? I have no one. All I have is my job, and the only man I might be interested in is my colleague. And he prefers men to women. How's that for irony?"

"Life is sometimes that way," Houston agreed.

The waitress came back with a couple of plates. She put them on the table. Houston eyed the heap of tiny, steaming meatballs. Claire watched him with amusement. "Never ate Raptor balls before?"

"Nope. I've had Raptor steaks and roasts but never testicles. I didn't realize they would be this small."

Claire broke out into loud laughter. "Testicles? Why would you think those are testicles?"

Houston felt like a fool. "When she said *balls,* I just assumed she meant testicles."

"Well, you assumed wrong. These are meatballs made from Raptor meat." She shook her head and laughed again. "Don't mind me laughing," she said when she calmed down. "I'm not laughing about you. You should have seen your face when you looked at your plate. That was priceless. I haven't laughed like this for a long time."

He was annoyed at first, but then he chuckled. "That's how a newcomer to Epsilon must feel. Everything is new and strange." He tasted the meat and found it quite tasty. "Not bad," he said.

"I told you they make descent food here. Of course, we'd be eating in this place even if they didn't. Nothing else around for miles."

Houston looked up when he heard the opening of the door and stopped eating for a moment. He recognized the five men and the woman who came in.

One of the men saw him also and headed for their table. "Hey, Houston, fancy finding you here." He looked at Claire. "And in the company of such a beautiful woman. By the way, your wife is with us, but I'm sure you've spotted her already." He tipped his helmet and walked back to the group.

Houston stared after him. His eyes met Tara's. Her face seemed whiter than usual, but that could have been the lighting. She looked past him at Claire, her eyes wide. Then she turned away.

"Your wife?" Claire said.

"She's not my wife. That is the woman I told you about. Her name is Tara."

"The one who is looking for her brother, that Gilbert Turner?"

Houston nodded and cursed himself for being such an idiot. He should have known better than to come here with another woman. This being the only place where people could find something to eat, it was only logical that Tara would show up with her new escort.

"I can see why you love her. She's beautiful and...young. Somehow, she looks familiar."

Houston chuckled grimly. "You've probably seen her before... years ago. In the mirror."

"Are you saying she looks like me?"

"Yes. Very much so."

Claire's smile was sad. "Too bad she came in here before I had a chance to seduce you. You would have been an easy target as vulnerable as you are right now. But perhaps not all is lost. She seems to have found a new man."

Houston looked back at the group of people waiting to be seated. Tara had her arm hooked into Lesage's arm.

Dr. Gilles Lesage. The gynecologist who had been doing more with his female patients than just look at their vaginas. Damn him.

As they walked by Houston's table, Tara threw a glance at Houston and smiled. Then she turned to Lesage and said something. The big prospector laughed and looked at Houston, waving as he did so.

Houston felt the urge to get up and smash his fist into the man's smug face. He heard Claire sigh across from him. "Must be nice to be in love," she said.

"Yeah, must be," he growled.

"She's not in love with that prospector. He could be her father. She loves you."

"If that is so than she has a strange way of showing it."

"She's trying to make you jealous. Believe me, I am a woman. I know. There is only one way to pay her back and that is to make *her* jealous." She touched his hand in an intimate gesture. "Of course I could be wrong about her still loving you. From what I can see you might have lost her already. That prospector may be older, but he is quite a handsome man. And she is young and horny."

"How would you know?"

"When I was her age, I was always horny. You know what they say about *Redheads*."

When he raised an eyebrow, she chuckled. "I wasn't married then. I met my husband here on Epsilon. He may have been a Preacher, but he was also quite a man. I think you know what I mean." She emptied her glass of wine. "By the way, are you still looking for her brother?"

He thought for a moment. "Yes, I am. That's what I came here for."

"I just remembered something. There is an old prospector who might know more about the people who came here around the time Turner did. I'll take you to him once we're finished eating."

He took a sip from his beer. Putting down the glass, he said, "I've lost my appetite."

"But I haven't," she said. "Now be a good boy and wait until I'm finished. At least, drink your beer. I'm going to have another glass of wine."

He drank his beer and ordered another one when she insisted. After drinking the second bottle he didn't feel so bad anymore.

Before they left the eatery, Clair went to the counter and picked up a couple of sandwiches and stuffed them into one of her pant pockets.

The old prospector lived inside *The Mound*. The entrance to it was barred by a metal gate to keep out predators. The road inside was pitted and full of depressions, not as smooth as the road inside Epsilon City, and walking on it could be treacherous.

"Old Benjamin lives on the fourth level. It's a bit of a climb."

"That's okay. I need the exercise."

Clair laughed softly and poked her elbow into his side. "I could think of much better exercise than climbing up this road."

After reaching the fourth level they turned into one of the side tunnels, not as well lit as the main tunnel, and Houston had to be careful not to step into the potholes. The only light came from the odd minisun attached to the low ceiling at irregular intervals.

"Here we are. He should be home. His days of roaming the jungle for treasures are over." She banged her fist on the door made from a sheet of thick plastic. "Bennie, are you in there? It's Claire from the Trading Commission."

"Of course I'm in," answered a raspy voice from the inside of the cave. "Where else would I be these days?"

Claire pushed open the flimsy door and walked in.

The walls of the cave were covered with mats woven from thin reeds to make them appear warmer and more pleasant. The room itself was furnished with benches and chairs made from Octopus tree roots.

The old man who sat in one of the chairs seemed to be busy studying some charts in the light of a torch clipped to the back of his chair. He squinted at them with rheumatic eyes and waved for them to come closer. "Have a seat. Rest your legs. I know they must ache after climbing up here."

Claire walked up to him and put her hand on his shoulder. "How are you coming along, Bennie?"

Benjamin chuckled merrily. "Fine, just fine. I'm planning an expedition into the area west of here. According to my charts there should be an abundance of green diamonds in the *Misty Plains* region."

"Well, maybe you'll be lucky this time, Bennie."

He cackled. "I have a good feeling about it." Putting his charts onto the small table beside him, he looked at her. "You didn't come here just to ask me how I was doing."

"No, I didn't. I have a friend who's looking for a prospector you might know. He came here about five years ago. His name is Gilbert Turner."

"Gilbert Turner? Hmm." The old man shook his head. "My memory isn't what it used to be, you know. Would you like a cup of tea? I've got some water boiling on the stove."

"Sure, if it's not too much trouble."

"No trouble. I don't get too many visitors these days. Only Marty comes by to bring me supplies and food. Everyone else seems to have died or disappeared, like the man you're looking for."

Benjamin got up from his chair and hopped to a portable stove on a counter. Houston realized the old man had only one leg.

"Did you say you are planning an expedition?" he asked.

"Yes, I am. Are you interested in coming along?" Benjamin gave Houston a questioning and, so it seemed, hopeful look.

"How many people are going?"

"So far there's only me, but I let out the word. They'll be coming to sign up as soon as it's official. Just like in the old days. You just wait and see. I still got it, you know."

"I'm sure you have," Houston said to humor the old man. He felt a wave of pity rising in him. *I hope I never end up like this.* "How did he loose his...?" he mouthed to Claire.

"Raptor," she whispered back.

"I filled the cups. Maybe you want to get them yourself. Be careful, the tea is hot," Benjamin said, hopping back to his chair. He picked up his charts and seemed to study them. Looking up, he said, "What did you say you wanted?"

"We are wondering if you remember Gilbert Turner," Claire said with a gentle voice.

"Am I supposed to know him?"

"We were hoping. You've been around for a long time."

"Yes, I have. Seen a lot of men and women die. Maybe this guy was one of them." He put his hand against his forehead. "I've had this humming in my head lately. Sounds like a swarm of bees." His face brightened suddenly. "Did you say Turner? Was his first name Gil?"

"That could be the one. What do you remember?"

"I remember a young man by that name. A redhead. Stocky feller. Very inquisitive. Wanted to know about the Commission. I remember him quite well. Took him into the jungle a couple of times, but that was some years ago. Haven't seen him since."

"Do you remember what happened to him?"

"He went north, to Raptors Tooth. I remember that. Apparently, someone found a large deposit of amethysts. Desert Hell wasn't much in those days."

"It's not much better these days I hear," Claire said, chuckling.

"Did I tell you that I was planning an expedition?" The old man went back to studying his charts. He pointed at a spot with a knobby finger. "Right here..."

"I'm sure you'll find it, Bennie. Thanks for the tea and information. Take care." Claire bent and kissed him on the cheek. She reached into her pocket and pulled out the sandwiches. "Here, I brought you something to eat."

He took the small package without looking at it. "It's there. I know it. I can feel it in my bones."

They left while he was still muttering to himself.

"Poor fellow." Houston said when they were in the tunnel outside. "He's living in a world all by himself. Can we trust his information?"

"Did he describe that Turner correctly?"

"He did."

"Well then, we can trust what he told us. Sometimes his memory is quite clear."

"When did he loose that leg?"

"A couple of years ago. He wasn't the same after that."

"You seem to be fond of him? What is he to you?"

"He's an old friend. He helped me get over the rough edges after my husband got killed." She rubbed one of her eyes. "It's dusty in these old tunnels. Let's get out of here."

Walking down the uneven surface of the road was easier then climbing it, but when they left The Mound and stepped into the open, they also stepped into the hot and humid air. "Amazing how cool it is inside that giant anthill," Houston remarked.

"Even thousands of years ago the primitive population was already quite adept at building their hives. Of course, they've evolved since then. I believe we are underestimating the Uur and the Queel," Claire said.

"I haven't had much contact with any of them. I've heard of the Queel, but I've never seen any."

"They are giant bees. I guess that would be the best way to describe them. They don't trade with us, unlike the Uur, who come to Lizard's Tongue quite often." She stopped and looked at her watch. "I don't feel like going back to the office, but I should go back. I don't want to antagonize Heller too much. He's a good employee and I wouldn't want him to quit because he's overworked. What are your plans for the rest of the day?"

He shrugged. "I don't have any."

"How about coming with me to the office and helping with moving some of the stuff that came with the bus today? My back and I will thank you later."

At first, he was going to say no but looking into her green eyes and pleading face made him laugh. "Okay. A little exercise might do me good. Tomorrow I'll be sitting in that damn bus again."

"Does that mean you are going to Desert Hell?"

"I'll follow the trail even further if I have to. I made a promise and I'm going to keep it."

"Even if the one you made the promise to rejects you?"

He nodded. "Even then."

She grabbed his arm and pulled him with her. "Men like you don't come along every day. That young woman is a fool if she doesn't hold onto you."

Heller raised an eyebrow when he saw them walking back into the office. He smirked when he addressed Claire, "Back already? It either didn't work out, or he is a fast one. Or maybe...is there hope?"

"Oh, shut up, Heller. Dave here is going to give you a hand moving all those boxes." She glared at him. "Let me warn you...he is not interested in you, okay?"

"What a shame." Heller rolled his eyes upward. "Isn't anybody anymore?"

Houston walked with Heller to one of the warehouses. Crates and boxes were stacked outside the door that led into the warehouse.

"This is a job for robots, not for Humans," Heller complained as he picked up the first box.

"Why don't you have any robots?"

"Apparently, the cost of sending and maintaining a robot does not warrant its presence here. An addition, the people in Epsilon City think we have nothing to do up here. They could at least send us a small air-sled to transport these heavy boxes. I'm not a muscle-bound hunk like...like you for instance." His eyes roamed over Houston. "You may not be very tall, but you sure have broad shoulders. I'll bet you're big all over." He leered. "You're sure you don't like men?"

"I'm quite sure." Houston laughed when Heller rolled his eyes again. "Now, let's get these boxes in there."

Claire came by a couple of hours later to check up on them and to help stacking some of the lighter boxes. "How about if you come over to my place tonight? I'll cook you a nice supper," she said when they were alone for a moment.

Houston knew that she had an ulterior motive. As tempting as her offer sounded, his conscience didn't allow him to accept. "I'd like to, but I need to talk to Tara tonight. She needs to know what we found out."

She nodded, disappointment clearly in her face. "If for some reason you should change your mind, I live in Apartment four. I'll be home."

"I think I'd better go. It is getting late. Thanks for a pleasant afternoon and for your help." He grabbed his backpack and walked away with heavy feet. He felt lousy about his decision and cursed himself for being such a stick-in-the-mud, but he would not have felt right about it. It didn't matter what he did, either of his decisions would leave him feeling rotten.

He went to the habitat that held the hostel. "I need a room for the night," he told the clerk behind the desk. The clerk nodded and handed him a key. Before he turned away, Houston asked, "Where can I find Miss Tara Turner?"

The clerk shrugged. "She's probably in the lounge."

"Thanks." Heading for the lounge, he ran into John Lamont. The little prospector nodded to him and asked, "What's up, Houston?"

"Is Tara with you guys?"

"She is, but let me give you some advice, Houston...don't bother looking for her."

"Why not?"

"She doesn't want to talk to you."

"She's my wife, damn it."

Lamont smiled, almost gently. "No, she isn't. She told us everything. No need to pretend anymore."

Houston let his shoulders droop. A heavy rock seemed to have taken up residence in his stomach.

I guess it's really over.

"You want to give her a message, Lamont?"

"Sure."

"Tell her that her brother might be in Desert Hell. I'll be going there with the bus tomorrow."

"I'll forward the message, but we know already about her brother. She's coming with us to Desert Hell. Maybe you shouldn't even bother coming, since you've managed to pick up another woman already. You sure didn't mourn the loss of your...your former wife for too long." He grinned and walked away.

"I only had dinner with that woman, that's all," Houston called after him. His feet were like lead when he walked down the corridor to his room. He threw his backpack onto the narrow bed, angry and disappointed. He needed to talk to someone before he went crazy. He knew only one person who would appreciate his presence and treat him with warmth, not with rejection. When he left the habitat, he checked the sky and scanned his surroundings out of habit, but his mind didn't register the dark shadow dropping on him until it was almost too late. Only his fast reflexes saved him from having his shoulders ripped open by the sharp claws of his attacker.

He heard the *swoosh...swoosh* of giant, leathery wings and swung around, his rifle flowing into his hands. Rolling out of harms way, he fired his rifle. The bright energy beam grazed the Dactyl's chest and burned a hole into one of its wings. The flying reptile screamed in defiance and dropped, hitting the hard ground with a loud thud. Flapping its wings, it tried to rise. Houston fired another shot into the wide chest. The acrid smell of charred flesh hung unpleasant in the air. With a dying screech the long head of the Dactyl slowly sank into the dust.

Houston watched as the light died in the great reptile's yellow eyes. Alert and cautious now, aware that Dactyls usually traveled in small groups, he searched the sky again, but it seemed this one had been a loner. Dusting off his clothing, he hurried toward the habitat that housed the office and residences of the Trading Commission.

Claire seemed surprised to see him. "I didn't expect you to come back. What changed you mind?"

He didn't say anything, just grabbed her and planted a rough kiss on her lips. At first, she struggled a little, but then she returned his kiss. When they separated, she gasped for air and gave a little laugh. "Wow, you must be angry about something."

He stared into her face. "I hope your offer was sincere."

"About cooking supper for you?" she said, smiling.

"We both know that's not what you meant." He took off his helmet and put it on the floor.

Claire regarded him silently. "I meant what I said," she said after a short pause. "Make yourself comfortable while I prepare something." She left and went into the kitchen, while he sat down on her small couch.

"Do you want something to drink?" she called from the kitchen.

"I'll have a cup of water, if you don't mind," he called back. "My throat is parched."

She came back a moment later and handed him a cup. "This is Fernapple juice," she said. "Better than plain water."

He heard her rummaging around in the kitchen and closed his eyes.

Tara, Tara, how could things have gone so wrong between us?

A warm hand touched his cheek. He opened his eyes and looked into a pair of green eyes. "Tara?" he said, but then he realized his mistake and murmured, "Sorry. I must have dozed off."

Claire laughed softly. "You've been asleep for two hours. I didn't want to wake you."

He sat up and rubbed his eyes. "I'm awake now. How about the food you promised?"

"That can wait. It's cold now anyway. I have something else in mind." She straddled his legs and sat in his lap, facing him.

He hadn't noticed it before, but she had taken off her clothes and was dressed only in a short, flimsy gown. Her breasts were clearly visible through the gauzy material.

Kissing him, she opened his shirt and exposed his chest. Then she ran her hands over his chest muscles. He kissed her back, lifted her gown, and put his hands on her naked buttocks. She moaned into his mouth and rubbed her pussy over his erection.

His penis was a hard rod inside his pants, and he knew there was no return from the road he had chosen. Her hands fumbled with his belt, trying to open it.

"Let me help," he groaned. He lifted her up so she could push down his pants past his knees. His erection jumped free and when he let her down again, she sheathed him with a loud cry. He slid into her creamy love-channel with a deep moan as the sweet pleasure rushed through his body.

He had been without a woman for much too long; he hardly remembered how it felt to have the hot, soft walls of a woman's vagina close around his rigid shaft. She whipped her pelvis back and forth with frantic movements; her soft buttocks clenched in his hands every time she pushed down.

"Why am I so horny?" he panted. "My penis feels like a rod of iron."

She chuckled. "It could be because I put a few drops of Mangaleeberry juice into you Fernapple drink. It's a powerful aphrodisiac."

"Why would you do that?" He grunted, holding on to her thrusting buttocks.

"Because you needed some cheering up and I needed a good fuck." Her chest heaved with the effort to get more air into her lungs and her fingers dug into his shoulders as she brought herself to her first orgasm. Crying out, she quivered in his lap and doused him with her warm liquid. "This feels wonderful. Try to hold back as long as you can. I need this badly," she sobbed.

"So do I." Moaning, he closed her mouth with his to stop her loud cries.

After a while she tired and slipped from his lap. Removing her gown, she lay down on the floor, her knees bent, and her legs spread wide. He got up from the couch and undressed, all the while studying her naked body. Her breasts were firm, hardly sagging on her ribcage, and the rest of her body was solid and nicely rounded in the right places.

"You are a beautiful woman," he told her. Then he chuckled. "And a devious one."

She looked at him through the tangle of red hair that had fallen across her face. Laughing, she put her foot against his chest, caressing him with her toes. "As much as I like to hear you giving me compliments, I want you to talk to me with your whole body not just your mouth." Her foot moved down to his erection. "Put that thing back into me before I get cold."

He grinned and slipped between her open thighs. After that they didn't speak; it was silent in the room, the only sounds their harsh breathing and their moans of pleasure.

[11]

DESERT HELL WAS ONLY ONE HUNDRED AND FIFTY MILES FROM LIZARD'S Tongue, but the road was not well maintained. Not every bus went as far as Desert Hell.

There wasn't much to see in this community. The people lived in mounds, similar to the one in Lizard's Tongue, only smaller and more primitive. The mounds were probably close to two hundred thousand years old, possibly older, their builders gone a long time ago. The jungle was kept back by hard, rocky ground and the desert that stretched eastward for a hundred miles.

When the bus drove into the settlement, Houston saw men riding animals the size of donkeys, flash rifles slung across their shoulders. It brought back memories of his time in the jungle when he had used a Boraz to carry his equipment. Those little animals were strong and dependable.

Looking around, he also saw a few trailers set up beside the small habitat that housed the office of the Trading Commission. It seemed the trailers were there to stay because some of their owners had piled rocks around theirs, probably to keep small predators from crawling underneath.

The bus stopped in front of the only habitat in town. As far as Houston knew, the hostel was the second building inside the dome.

The drive from Lizard's Tongue had been awkward. When he boarded the bus, Tara gave him a cold stare and then she turned away. She sat beside Lesage the whole time and seemed to be comfortable among the prospectors.

He didn't try to talk to her, feeling guilty about what he had done in Lizard's Tongue. It had felt right when he lay in the arms of Claire. She had been passionate and loving, and given him something he thought he needed, but when he sat in the bus and watched Tara, he felt rotten. He had refused her and then betrayed her with another woman.

Had he accepted Tara's offer that night they both might have regretted it in the morning. His conscience had not allowed him to take advantage of her drunken state, but now she felt rejected. Whatever he didn't do or did, it was the wrong thing.

To Hell with her! To Hell with this whole stinking planet! If I ever find a way off this freaking place, I'll be glad to take it.

The five prospectors and the other passengers began unloading their luggage from the trailer. The prospectors left, carrying their luggage on their backs. Tara left with them. Houston waited until most of them were finished before he unloaded his stuff. He put everything into a neat pile. Some of the things were meant for Tara's use, but she would probably not claim them. It didn't matter. He had paid for everything anyway. One of the items among his possessions was a *glider*, a flat platform that floated on a magnetic field to carry all the stuff he brought with him. He unfolded and activated it. Then he loaded all the boxes and bags onto its surface.

"That is a smart idea. I wish I would have thought of that," one of the other passengers said.

Houston looked up from his task and said, "It makes transporting my luggage a little easier."

"I'll say. Oh, by the way, my name is Emmeril Zogar. What happened to that cute redhead I saw you with?"

"She's decided to change company," Houston said, trying to sound flippant but not quite succeeding in his attempt.

Zogar chuckled. "Yeah, I know how that is. Women can be fickle. I haven't seen you before on this bus. With all the stuff you're bringing, I guess this is your first time in Desert Hell."

"Yes, it is. Actually, I'm looking for someone. His name is Gilbert Turner."

The man pulled on his goatee and screwed up his face. "Can't say I've heard of him...but then I've only been here for a couple of years. Men come and go. Not many stay for long. I've been thinking of moving on. Maybe he went further north...if he is still alive." He turned away and called to one of his friends, "Hey, Kirby, have you ever heard the name Gilbert Turner?"

The other man put down the large pack he was carrying and came over. "The name sounds familiar. Not the last name but the first. Gilbert...everyone called him Gil. Short, stocky feller. He and Geraldine used to be an item, but I haven't seen him around for years. She's living with a guy by the name of Buckert right now."

Houston felt a slight shiver of excitement. It seemed he was finally getting a bit closer. "Do you remember if this Gil had red hair?"

"Yep, he did. Carrot-red hair. His beard too."

"This Geraldine...is she still around?"

"She certainly is. I can take you to her if you want."

"I would appreciate that very much. Do you think it's safe to leave my stuff here?"

Kirby grinned. "I wouldn't leave it out of my sight, friend. This is Desert Hell. Things are a little wild here sometimes. Take my advice...bring everything with you. By the way, I saw that redheaded beauty with Lesage. What happened? I thought she was with you."

"She was." Houston shrugged, spreading his hands in a nonchalant gesture. "Changed her mind."

"With Lesage? With her looks she can do better."

Houston gave him a crooked grin. "Exactly my thinking, but who understands women, right?"

"That's why I never hooked up with one," Zogar said. He looked at Houston's glider. "Say, since we're going in the same direction, how about letting us put our stuff on your glider?"

"Sure, go ahead."

Houston followed the two men, pulling his loaded glider behind him. The sun stood high in the sky and burned with merciless fire. Houston wiped the sweat from his forehead, feeling the gritty sand, which was carried by a hot wind blowing from the desert, scratch his skin.

He spit and cursed.

Zogar, who walked beside him, carrying his flash rifle in both hands, laughed. "Are you beginning to understand why they call this place *Desert Hell*?"

"I thought it was because of all the *Devil-hogs* in the area," Houston puffed. "I saw a small pack of them on the outskirts before we arrived here."

"They're here, plus the Raptors, the Dactyls, and a score of other nasty critters." He scanned the air and the desert with narrow eyes. "Take my advice, friend. Never let down your guard and keep your rifle ready at all times."

"Thanks." Houston remembered his near fatal encounter the day before with the Dactyl in Lizard's Tongue. Quick reflexes and a good portion of luck had saved his skin, probably his life. "I have to get used to this again. I've spent too many years in the safety of Epsilon City."

"The city has grown since I was there last," Kirby said. "Couldn't live there. Too many restrictions. I prefer this place." He whistled and pointed with his rifle. "Watch out. A couple of Dactyls might decide to drop in for a visit."

Houston looked into the sky and saw the familiar silhouettes of two flying reptiles. They were still far away, but they could cover the distance in a short time. He gripped his flash rifle tighter and kept his eyes and attention on them.

Kirby called out to one of the men on Boraz-back. "Hey, Hopper, have you seen Geraldine?"

"I saw her yesterday. She should be home." The man grinned. "Are you planning to visit her? I hear Buckert is out on the trail somewhere."

Kirby grinned back. "Wouldn't take the chance. This feller here wants to talk to her."

"Well, take care. I'm on my way out." Hopper pointed a thumb at the second Boraz walking beside him. "Had to get myself another pack-carrier. Lost the last one to a hungry croc. Almost got me too."

"Good hunting. We'll probably be heading out in a couple of days."

They stopped in front of one of the mounds. "She's in there. Good luck." The two men removed their gear from Houston's glider and left.

He stood looking at the entrance to the mound. It was barred with a gate made from iron. Uncertain how to open the gate, he found a latch and lifted it. It swung open, and he pulled his glider through the gate into the narrow tunnel, closing the gate behind him. The tunnel was lit by a minisun glued against the ceiling. As he walked past a door, it opened, and a woman looked out. When she saw him, she smiled and said, "Are you the new guy who's moving into Justin's place?"

"No, I'm afraid not. I'm looking for Geraldine."

"Oh." She gave him a puzzled look. "Anything happened to Buckert? Are you moving in with her?"

He chuckled. "No to that question also. I just got here from Epsilon City. I'm looking for someone she might know."

"I see. She lives in unit three." She tilted her head and pulled her lips into a seductive smile. "If you have nothing better to do, why don't you stop by later? My man has been gone for almost a month now and I feel kinda lonely."

"Thank you for the offer but I must pass. Sorry."

"I'm sorry too. You look like a guy a woman could feel comfortable with." She gave him another smile and closed the door.

He walked on until he got to unit three. The door was closed so he knocked and waited. The woman, who opened it, stared at him. "Who are you? Anything happened to Buckert?"

"Sorry to bother you, Ma'am. Nothing happened to Buckert, as far as I know. My name is Dave Houston. I was told by Kirby that you might be able to help me."

"Help you?" She looked at him with suspicion in her brown eyes. "I'm not that kind of a woman, even if there are rumors."

"I know nothing about any rumors." He smiled. "I understand you knew a man by the name of Gilbert Turner."

"Gil?" Her eyes were large. "Is he dead?"

"I don't know. I'm looking for him. Do have any idea where I might find him?"

She brushed her hand over her eyes. "Why don't you come in? I don't like talking in the corridor. Too many busy ears, you know." Stepping aside, she let him walk past her.

He looked around and was surprised by the spacious room. The bright light of a minisun took away the gloom usually found in these small caves. It was easy to see the female touch in the placement of furniture and little knickknacks standing around. Nothing was fancy, but the place looked clean and maintained.

"Sit down." She took her own seat on a bench woven from tree roots and watched him as he sat down on a chair made from the same material. "How do you know Gil?" she asked, fiddling with her fingers.

"Oh, no, you misunderstand. I don't know him at all. His sister is the one looking for him. She just arrived on Epsilon, and I offered to help her."

"Where is she?"

"With some friends."

"Here?"

"Yes."

"Who are these friends?" She seemed suddenly uneasy and suspicious.

"Gilles Lesage, Redge Dallas, John Lamont..."

She stopped him. "I know them. They're all right. They'll take good care of her."

I bet they will. He remembered how they had behaved in Epsilon City, drinking and celebrating for two days and nights. They may not be young in years, but they certainly had shown plenty of stamina with the *Girls of the Night*. "I was told you knew Turner."

"*Knew* him?" She laughed. "Yes, I knew him. We lived together for almost a year. He was gone most of the time and I got tired of waiting for him. A woman gets lonely here." She paused and stared into thin air. "He was a good man, though. Many times, I wished I had been more patient. When he came back the last time, I was living with someone else." She shrugged and smiled. "I have needs like every woman and there are plenty of single men here who are willing to keep a lonely woman company."

"Men get lonely too," Houston said with a low voice. "And a man has needs just like a woman." His heart suddenly ached for Tara's company. *I wonder what she is doing right now.*

"You sound like a man who has been spending too much time alone," she said, studying him from under lowered lashes. "Anything I can do?"

"You can tell me where I might find Gilbert Turner," he said, his gaze on her heaving breasts.

She saw his gaze and smiled. "I was hoping you would ask for more." Sighing, she touched her earlobe. "He gave me these earrings when we first met. Told me they belonged to his mother. I loved him for that alone. No man gives away his mother's earrings lightly." She shook her head and looked at him with sad eyes. "I have no idea what happened to him. He went north, that's all I can tell you."

"What's up north?"

"Another mining town. What else?"

"I guess that's where I'll go," he said and rose. "Thank you for your information."

"I'm sorry I can't be of more help. I'd be willing to make it up to you."

He shook his head. "I made one mistake already. I'm not going to make another one, as tempting as it is. You're a lovely woman. I can see why Turner gave you those earrings. I would have done the same." He walked to the door and opened it. Before he walked out, he said, "I hope you can fill that lonely spot in your heart." Then he closed the door behind him.

In these places any woman looks lovely, even if she is as plain as Geraldine. Women like to hear a man say, "You're beautiful". I should have told Tara that more often. It would not have been a lie.

155

Pulling his glider with his possessions behind him, he headed for the habitat to claim a room in the hostel for the night. He needed to get more information about the communities further north and how to get there. He might have to purchase a Boraz or find some other means of travel.

The wind blowing from the desert had gained in strength, and he hunched his shoulders to protect his face from the bombardment of fine sand. When he heard voices, he looked up and saw a group of men coming out of one of the mounds; he recognized Lesage and Dallas. He also saw Tara with them. The group seemed to have spotted him and headed in his direction. He wasn't sure if he should acknowledge them or just walk on. The men suddenly stopped and waved their hands over their heads, staring and yelling at him. He didn't know what they were yelling about because of a sudden noise in the air. Then they all lifted their rifles, aiming them in his direction.

Too late he recognized the danger.

Something heavy slammed into him from behind and knocked him to the ground. His face hit the rocks. He fought to stay conscious but bright flashes and black spots kept blinking like a strobe light in front of his eyes.

———

When he regained his awareness and opened his eyes, he saw nothing but darkness.

I can't see. I'm blind!

Panic struck him, but then he realized that he lay facedown under something heavy that kept him pinned to the ground and his face pressed into the sand. Turning his head, he saw light through a crack between him and whatever lay on top of him. He also saw boots moving back and forth.

"Let's get this thing off of him," someone yelled.

"I hope he isn't dead," someone else said. He thought he recognized Elbenheim's deep voice. Then he heard a woman's loud sob, but he wasn't sure. His head hurt and his face burned.

"Anders, Redge, help me lift up this wing. John, you try to pull him out."

He felt the weight above him getting lighter, and then someone reached in and grabbed his arm. Another pair of hands got hold of his shirt.

"Damn! He seems to be stuck. Can't you lift any higher?"

He tried to move his legs and found they moved a little. His boots were digging into the ground, and he used the little leverage he had to push himself forward. Slowly he felt his body move.

"Let me help you," a voice called. The thing above him moved higher and suddenly he slid out from under it.

"I think he's alive."

Hands touched his shoulder. "Don't move in case you've got broken bones."

"I think I'm okay," he croaked, coughing up dust. He turned onto his back and lay there, wondering if he really was okay. He didn't feel any pain, but he knew that would come later.

"Oh, my god, look at his face. It's all bloody," a woman cried out. She knelt beside him and stroked his hair. "Please, don't die, please... please..."

His vision began to clear, and he recognized Tara's tearstained face. "I don't die that easily," he said. "Sorry to disappoint you."

She shook her head and smiled through her tears. "This is all my fault. I'm so sorry I behaved the way I did. I love you, Dave."

"I thought you loved Lesage."

She laughed between tears. "Lesage? Don't be silly. He's like my father to me."

"I'm not that old," Lesage protested, bending down to look at Houston. "How are you feeling? You look like Hell."

Houston looked at Tara. "I'm feeling much better already. I love you, too, Tara." He moved his legs and arms. "I'd like to stand up. I think I'm lying on a couple of rocks, and they're digging into my back."

"He's fine," Tara said, laughing and sobbing. "He's already complaining."

Groaning, he sat up and wiped the back of his hand across his mouth. When he looked at it, he saw blood smeared all over his hand.

"It's your nose," Tara said. "You must have banged it when you hit the ground. You're not a pretty sight."

"What the Hell happened?" He stared at the thing lying in front of him. At first, he thought it was a Dactyl, by when he looked closer he saw it wasn't. He had never seen a flying reptile of its type. "What is that?"

"One of the desert-fliers," Lesage said. "They don't come in often. Actually never. They don't like the jungle. This one must have lost its way. Luckily, it's a young one otherwise you'd be dead now. The adults are twice the size and more vicious. Someone dubbed them *Desert-eagles*, even though they bear no resemblance to an eagle."

Houston shuddered when he looked at the dead reptile. It didn't have a long beak like a Dactyl, but a short, almost round, thin one with the upper jaw overlapping the bottom part on each side. No teeth, only sharp blades that could take a man's head off with one chomp.

"Even though they're huge, their wings are strong enough so they can take off from the ground, unlike the Dactyls, who launch themselves off high perches and sail the wind currents," Lamont said.

Houston stood up and dusted off his clothing. He realized his helmet was gone and looked for it. Then he saw all his belongings strewn all over the ground. One of the reptile's wings had knocked them off the glider, which was half-buried under the long wing. "Got to get my stuff together," he said, "but first I need to free the glider."

"I'll give you a hand," Lesage said.

Fortunately, the part of the reptile that lay across the glider was just the tip of the wing and he had no trouble lifting it up. After the glider was free, Houston began loading his belongings back onto it.

"They're not bad eating," one of the men who had come to help said. "Maybe we should start butchering it before the scavengers come."

"I'll agree. Let's get some guys together. We'll have to get rid of the carcass either way."

Tara came up to Houston and touched his hand. When he looked at her, she smiled shyly. Then, with a loud sob, she put her arms around his neck. "I'm just so glad you're okay. I don't know what I would have done had I lost you."

He held her tight. "I thought I lost you," he said with a low voice.

"Never. I admit you hurt my feelings when you refused me, and I was mad at you. Mad and disappointed. And a little bit embarrassed." She gave a little chuckle. "Maybe mostly embarrassed. I thought you didn't love me. I wanted to make you jealous, but then I realized I was wrong. I was ready to come back to you and then I saw you with that woman. What happened between you and her?"

"Nothing happened," he lied. There was nothing gained by telling her the truth. If he did, he would lose her for sure. This time it would be real. He had no feelings for Claire. She had scratched an itch and that was that. "We had lunch. I needed company."

"Oh, Dave, can you forgive me for what I did?"

"You were drunk, Tara. There is nothing to forgive. I refused you because I love you." He smiled gently. "It was not a painless decision, believe me. It would have been so easy to give in."

She touched his cheek. "I was a fool. I promise I will never leave you again. But you look horrible. Come, let's get you cleaned up."

"I still have to check into the hostel," he said. He could feel a sudden dull pain in his shoulder. "And I need to take some painkillers. By the way, I have some news about your brother. I'll tell you everything later."

———

They discovered there was a place in the hostel that served simple meals. The owner apologized for the lack of variety. "Our Food Processor is not one of those sophisticated modern ones. We can't afford one." He lifted his pudgy shoulders in an apologetic gesture. "We don't get too many customers in here because of our location."

"No need to apologize," Houston said. "We're happy you're serving anything at all." He and Tara were the only customers in the place. All of the other passengers on the bus had been residents of Desert Hell and had their own places to live.

"How long are you two staying?" the proprietor asked.

"I don't think for very long," Houston said. "Our next destination lies north. One of the mining communities. We just don't know yet which one."

"There is nothing much north of here. A few camps, the largest and furthest one, about two hundred miles from here, is called Raptor's Tooth. The roads are bad, and you can get yourself lost unless you have someone with you who knows the area."

"Do you know someone?"

The proprietor shrugged. "I heard that Emmeril Zogar's been talking about pulling up stakes and trying his luck further up north."

"Zogar. Funny you should mention him," Houston said, surprised. "I've met him. He was on the bus with us."

"Maybe you should talk to him. He might be persuaded to come along with you. He's a good man. Knows the jungle and how to survive in it."

"Thank you for the advice. We will certainly follow up on it."

"No trouble. I'd better get back and get your food. Would you mind if I join you? I don't get much chance to talk to anybody."

"Be our guest. Perhaps you can tell us more about Desert Hell."

Tara watched the pudgy man shuffle toward the kitchen. "Must be lonesome living in this desolate place without a close friend. Why does anybody who isn't a prospector even stay here?"

"Why does anyone stay on Epsilon?" Houston countered.

Tara looked at him and reached across the table. "I am so happy to be with you again. It was plain agony watching you but not being able to talk to you. I never realized how much I love you."

"And I never realized how much you mean to me. We've only known each other for such a short time, but I've grown to love you," he said gently, holding her hand. "I love you with all my heart, Tara."

Her green eyes sparkled with happiness when she gazed at him. "You don't know what it means to me to hear you say that," she said, tears rolling down her cheeks. She rose from her seat and came around the table to sit on his lap. Then she kissed him with great passion, and he held her tightly in his arms, not willing to let her go.

They broke apart when someone coughed delicately beside

them. Houston looked up at the proprietor who smiled down at them. "I thought you two were hungry?" He carried a couple of plates with steaming food in his hands.

Tara laughed and slid off Houston's lap. "We're celebrating," she said happily, and moved back to her seat.

"Celebrating?" He gave her a wink. "If I'd be lucky enough to have a beautiful woman like you even look at me, I'd be celebrating also." He put the plates down in front of them. "Enjoy. I'll be back in a moment with my food."

They both laughed.

"I guess we'd better wait till he comes back," Tara said. Tasting a little bit from her food, she said, "It doesn't even taste bad. Some kind of stew I think."

"It probably isn't meat since it comes from a Food Processor, but what the heck, as long as it tastes good. I only wished we could have some real wine to go along with it," Houston said.

The proprietor came shuffling back. He must have heard Houston's last remark. "No wine, I'm afraid. Just plain water. Fortunately, there is no shortage of water since we're still close enough to the jungle. We have a well that produces good clean water without the need to filter it." He settled his body into one of the four chairs and started eating. "Perhaps tomorrow we can have some real meat. I heard they shot an *Eagle* today," he said around a mouthful of stew.

"I heard the same thing," Houston said, aware of the pain in his shoulder again. "News travels fast here, I guess."

"It does. Most of it is hardly ever good. This place wasn't named *Desert Hell* for nothing."

"Why are you staying here?" Tara asked.

"Good question. I ask myself that every day when I sit alone in my room. Frankly, I don't really have an answer. I came her six years ago when someone found a great number of large diamonds just lying around in the sand at the edge of the desert. There was a rush of prospectors and fortune hunters setting up camp. The mounds made a perfect place to live in comparative safety."

"You've been here for six years already?"

He nodded. "I never found any diamonds. It turned out once the diamonds in that one spot had been mined there were no more, but there are plenty of other gems to be found in this area. When the Trading Commission put up this habitat and they needed someone to run the hostel, I applied for the job." He chuckled. "The safest place in Desert Hell. After I lost my partner to a pack of Raptors, I didn't go out anymore. I got scared. So here I am. Still here after six years." He looked at Tara. "Why are *you* here?"

"I'm looking for my brother."

"He is here in Desert Hell?"

"No, but he was."

"What's his name?"

"Gilbert Turner."

The pudgy man put down his fork and stared at her. "Gil? He was your brother?"

"Yes." Her eyes showed her sudden fear. "He *is* my brother. Do you know him?"

He nodded slowly and kept looking at her. "I should have seen the resemblance. He had red hair like you. And your features...the same eyes, the same high cheekbones. I should have seen that. But then...what are the chances? Aside from the fact it's been a while since I saw him."

"Do you know where I can find him?"

"Sorry. I don't even know if he is still alive. It's been nearly four years since I saw him last. Went north, that's all I know."

Her shoulders sagged with disappointment. "And here I was getting my hopes up. Doesn't anybody ever come back?"

"Sure, they do. To get supplies or trade in the gems they found, but they rarely stop here in Desert Hell, unless they want to say hello to someone. There is nothing they can buy here. You might have more luck to get information in Lizard's Tongue."

"We couldn't find anything there. They have no records of him other than what you've told us."

"That means nothing. Sometimes, for whatever reason, prospectors won't give their real name when they trade for stuff. Don't give up. Just because nobody has heard from him doesn't mean he is dead. He might be living in Raptor's Tooth, who knows. He used to live with Geraldine Laymon. She's still around. Maybe you should talk to her."

"I already talked to her," Houston said. "She told me the same thing you did. That's why we're heading north."

Houston held Tara close as they walked back to their room. She put her head against his shoulder, her arm around his waist. When the door closed behind them, she came into his arms and looked into his face. "I'd like to apologize again for the way I behaved," she said. "I was such a fool."

"Maybe I was the fool," he said, stroking her back. "What sane man refuses a beautiful woman who asks him to make love to her? Only a foolish man does that."

She smiled. "I can't argue with that. But maybe you did the right thing. I was drunk."

"You are not drunk now."

"No, I'm not. I know exactly what I'm doing." She lifted up and kissed him. After breaking the kiss, she said, "I love you, Dave, and you said you loved me too. When two people are in love they do more than just kiss. I want to do more than kiss you. I want to make love to you."

He didn't answer. Pulling her against him again, he kissed her hungrily. Then, without breaking the kiss, he lifted her shirt and put his hand over her breast. She moaned and fumbled with the belt on his pants. Sneaking a hand down his belly, she found his erection and stroked it.

Groaning, he released her. "Don't make me come like that," he panted. "I don't want to waste anything. Take off your clothes. I need to feel your naked body against mine."

They both undressed in a hurry and moved to the bed. Naked, she lay down and looked up at him with wide eyes, her chest heaving in anticipation, and her lips slightly open. Her arms reached for him. "Come, my darling, let's forget about everything for a while, and pretend we are in a place where there is nothing but peace and love."

"We are in that place right now," he said, smiling. Then he joined her on the bed and took her into his arms again. This time it felt good and right. There would be no regrets. When their bodies slipped together, she heaved a loud sigh. "You can't imagine how I dreamed about this moment," she whispered, her body trembling.

———

When he awoke in the morning and found Tara in his arms, he thought for an insane moment that he was still dreaming.

She stirred and opened her eyes. Her lips formed a smile, and she touched his face. "You are really here," she whispered.

"Yes, I am." He kissed her gently. "I will never leave you again. I love you so much, Tara."

"I love you too, darling." She stretched and yawned. Sitting up, the cover slipped down exposing her breasts. "Oops," she said, looking at him with a wicked smile.

He reached up to cup one of her breasts with his hand. "A little late to be modest, isn't it?" He chuckled. "You know, you are a bit of a tease, but I love that. You can't imagine how much self-control it took for me not to take you in my arms and let my hands roam all over your delectable body when you stood naked in front of me in that park in Camp Diamond." He laughed, almost embarrassed to admit it. "In fact, I wanted to do it the first time I saw you in the bus."

Her laughter teased him. "You know what you are? A lecherous old man."

"Old man? I must correct you, little lady. I'm only four years older than you."

Tousling his hair with her fingers, she giggled. "Is that four *Standard* years or four *Dawson-years*?"

"What's the difference?" He knew but he wanted to hear her answer.

"Well, *Dawson-years* are much longer, I'm sure you know. According to *Dawson-years* I am only five years old. That, my darling, makes you an old man, since you are already twenty-nine years old, and I am still a child."

He shook his head. "Twenty-nine *Standard* years, my child. You can't compare using different measurements."

She came close and pressed her breasts into his face. "I can."

He put his arms around her naked torso and put her onto her back. Her legs opened and he slid between them. She wriggled her lower body and captured his growing erection between her thighs. "I think you have something in mind," she whispered, her breath coming in little gasps.

Closing her mouth with his, he eased his hard penis into her welcoming love channel. She let out a loud moan and moved against him, milking him forcefully.

They thrashed on the bed like two wild beasts. Neither could get enough of the other one. Releasing their passion with loud cries, they collapsed into each other's arms and lay gasping for breath.

"You'll kill me before we get married," he groaned.

She lifted her head and looked at him. "You've never mentioned marriage before," she said.

"I am now. You don't really think I'm going to let a hot woman like you ever get away from me again?" He stroked her hair. "I love you with all my heart and I want to spend the rest of my life with you...as my wife."

He could see the tears forming in her eyes. "Oh, David, I was hoping you'd say that, but I didn't dare for fear of losing you. Not every man wants to get married."

"I want to get married. Will you marry me?"

Laughing happily, she kissed him on the lips. "Of course I will."

"We'd better get up before I'll succumb to your charms again," he said, holding her tight for a moment.

An hour later, washed and dressed, they headed for the dining room. After breakfast Houston asked the proprietor where he could find Emmeril Zogar.

The prospector was surprised and happy to see him. "I heard about your encounter with the Desert-eagle. You're a lucky man." He squinted at him. "What can I do for you?"

"I'm planning to head for Raptor's Tooth. I was wondering if you'd be interested in guiding us. The proprietor from the hostel hinted you might."

Zogar shook his head. "I've been thinking about getting away from Desert Hell, but not yet. My friend Brady found a promising place with some nice rubies. We'll be heading there in a couple of days."

"Do you know of anyone who might be interested?"

"Sorry, I don't."

Houston walked away, disappointed and frustrated. Going alone was out of the question. He would never put Tara in danger. When he told Tara, she said, "Don't give up, Dave. Something will come up. We'll just wait."

Despite the danger of being attacked by some hungry reptile, he and Tara went outside to look around. The wind was blowing again from the west, bringing with it the dry air of the desert, but also sand and more heat.

"How can people live here?" Tara asked, adjusting the breather mask over her mouth and nose.

"When you're desperate and have no other place to live, you stay wherever hope for a better life lies. You adjust and tell yourself it will get better." Houston stared into the hazy sky. It was pregnant with dust, obscuring the bright sun. He agreed with Tara. This was not a desirable location, but Humans adapted and fought against all odds, trying desperately to tame the environment, sometimes winning but much of the time losing the battle.

They went back into the habitat and searched out the dining room. "At least it's cool and comfortable in here," Tara said as they waited for the proprietor to bring their food.

He was about to reply when a woman's voice behind him said, "Hello there. It is nice to see fellow strangers in this place." Turning his head, his gaze fell on the woman who had spoken. She wasn't alone and when he looked at the man with her, he was a bit shocked and surprised to see him here of all places on Epsilon.

"Chief Stonewall," he said. "What the Hell are you doing in this forsaken place?"

The big Scout seemed as surprised as he. "Mr. Houston. We meet again."

Houston smiled. "I hope you didn't come here to find me."

"No. You are not the reason we are here." Stonewall returned the smile. "Just for your information, I am not the Chief of Epsilon City anymore." He shook Houston's hand. "Do you mind if we join you at your table?"

"Not at all."

Before Stonewall sat down, he said, "By the way, this is Demi."

"Pleased to meet you, Demi," Houston said. He looked at Stonewall. "What brings you here?"

"We are on our way to Raptor's Tooth."

"What a coincidence. So are we," Houston said with a glance at Tara.

"Why?"

"To find Tara's brother."

[12]

ACCEPTING MASTER SCOUT STONEWALL'S OFFER TO TRAVEL NORTH with them in the tank was the best thing they could have done, since there wasn't anyone in Desert Hell who seemed interested in guiding them. When Stonewall's offer came along, he didn't hesitate.

Demi, the woman, wasn't Stonewall's only companion. With him were Peters, another Scout, Houston had met him also already in Epsilon City, and a Union Trooper. His name was Mendez and he seemed to be the personification of the perfect soldier. Houston was not particularly fond of him. Of course, he had never been fond of any military man.

"Well, we've wasted another day in that desolate place," the Trooper said as they pulled away from Desert Hell.

"I wanted to find out if anyone knew about what the hell is going on in Raptor's Tooth. I don't like to drive into a situation blind," Stonewall said, his irritation quite obvious. "Especially since we encountered that unidentified object in the sky."

Houston knew what the big Scout meant. He and the others with him had seen an aircraft fly across the road a couple of hours before they reached Desert Hell. They didn't give him any details about the encounter. "That object you mentioned could have been one of the new fliers some of the small mining companies brought in," he suggested.

"According to the tank's computer it was of unknown origin," Stonewall said. "We're worried that the reptilian races are showing an interest in Epsilon."

"May I remind you that you are giving away military secrets to a civilian," Mendez said.

"Don't be absurd." Stonewall shook his head in obvious disgust. "Who is he going to tell? The Spiders?"

"That is not the point," Mendez growled. "We have three civilians on board who have their own interests. They might even be spies for the Belters. I'm still not sure about Safire. I wish he would have come along so I could keep an eye on him. Who knows what mischief he is going to cause in Desert Hell."

Houston gave a strangled laugh, feeling a sudden twinge of panic rising in him, knowing that Tara and her brother had come to Epsilon to spy for the Belters. "For your information...I was born on Earth," he said.

"What about your lady friend?"

"She came here to look for her brother. She has no interest in politics."

"You didn't answer my question. I want to know where she was born, since you brought up your origin."

"I was born on Dawson," Tara said.

"On Dawson. Well, well...you're a Belter."

"That doesn't make me a spy," she said with a defiant voice. "Besides, what is there to spy about on this planet? Everyone knows there are giant mushrooms growing everywhere. The jungle is populated with ferocious lizards the size of buildings. Prospectors are searching for precious gems and are eaten by the lizards in the process. What else is there? Oh..." She hit her forehead with her flat hand. "How can I forget? There are criminals in Epsilon City who kidnap young women and feed them to newly hatched Spiders who should have died a long time ago."

Houston put his hand on Tara's hand. "Don't bring that up now, please. It will only upset you. And me."

She squeezed his hand. "It's all right. I've come to terms with what happened there. I'm only trying to make a point."

"You are indeed making a point, lady," Mendez said. "You are in possession of knowledge that is dangerous to have. I'll be watching you."

"I didn't ask to be kidnapped."

"I'm sure you didn't, but it happened and in the process, you ended up with information you should never mention to anyone," Mendez growled.

"I'm quite confident Miss Turner's knowledge about the Spider eggs is not something she is going to broadcast to the Galaxy right now. Neither will we," Stonewall said. "I suggest you stick with watching the road, Mendez. In fact, it might be a good idea to stop and let those dinosaurs cross the road before we are trampled by them."

Mendez cursed under his breath and brought the tank to a halt. A group of large herbivorous dinosaurs lumbered across the road. The behemoths didn't pay any attention to the metal intruder that dared to come close enough to be crushed by them should they choose to do so.

"They sure are big," Tara whispered as if afraid they might hear her.

"Are you certain they can't see us in here?" Demi asked, her voice as low as Tara's. "This transparent dome gives me the shivers. It seems there is nothing but air above me."

"It's an illusion. I assumed you were used to it by now," Stonewall said.

"I don't think I can ever get used to this."

"You'd better get used to it because soon you'll be meeting these beasts in the open without a protective barrier between you and them," Mendez said, chuckling gleefully.

The last of the behemoths disappeared in the jungle and the tank rolled on again. Riding in a tank was different from sitting in a more comfortable bus, even though the passengers inside the tank were protected from being tossed around by a magnetic field that cut in as soon as conditions outside became rough.

The road was not as well traveled as the one from Epsilon City to Lizard's Tongue, and not nearly as good as the road to Desert Hell. Houston had never been this far up north before, and he was surprised to see different vegetation popping up between the mushroom trees. Some trees looked like the conifers on Earth, except these were growing much taller than any he ever saw on Earth.

He was quite happy to travel inside a tank instead of riding a Boraz. Having experienced the jungle before, he might have been able to do it, but he had his doubts about Tara.

Since the tank didn't have enough storage space, they were forced to leave much of their gear behind in Desert Hell, but Houston was confident that they would be able to survive with the stuff he had been able to bring. A change of clothing, hygienic products, and other necessary articles for their daily needs and, of course, spare power packs for the weapons and other equipment.

It was only approximately two hundred miles to Raptor's Tooth, but the tank traveled slowly, and it would take them a couple of days to get there...if everything went smoothly. It was still faster than on Borazback or walking. Apparently, there were a few scooters used by some prospectors, but Houston hadn't seen any yet. Not even in Desert Hell. Scooters tended to brake down. It was much safer to use a Boraz. Those little animals were more dependable and did provide some protection against the smaller lizards.

He was tired from the night before. Smiling, he leaned back and closed his eyes. Tara had not given him much chance to rest. She had seemed insatiable...not something he had minded.

"We should be in the first camp soon."

Houston opened his eyes when he heard one of the Scouts talking. Realizing it was Peters, he asked, "How long have we been traveling?"

"About three hours," Peters said. He chuckled. "Sorry to wake you. You've missed all the fun."

"What fun?"

Tara reached across the isle and touched his arm. "Only a pack of hungry Raptors that tried to attack the tank," she said. "Nothing to worry about...according to our friendly guide Trooper Mendez."

When Houston looked at the jungle on either side nothing seemed to have changed. It appeared they hadn't moved at all since the last time he looked. The jungle always looked the same. The trail ahead was barely noticeable. A man traveling through these parts could easily walk in the wrong direction.

The trail ended suddenly in a large, cleared area. All of them held their breath, even Mendez, when they surveyed the place that had once been a mining camp.

There was nothing left but charred, fused remnants of the tiny individual habitats the prospectors used in the temporary camps. They were supposed to be impervious to any known conventional weapons, but these looked as if they'd been smashed with a giant sledgehammer and then melted with a flamethrower.

They didn't see any survivors of the carnage that had been caused here, except for bits and pieces of gnawed bones.

When the tank neared the first habitat, a swarm of small scavengers scampered away, but moved only as far as the next habitat to glare and hiss at the newcomer who dared to challenge their claim to the banquet. A skull lay on top of a trampled mushroom, grinning at them.

"What the hell happened here?" Stonewall cursed loudly.

Houston had witnessed death and destruction before, but this was so horrific it took all his willpower not to get sick. He looked at Tara who sat white-faced in her seat just staring outside.

"Who would do such a thing?" Demi whispered.

"This is an act of war," Mendez said grimly.

"I wouldn't be so hasty in saying that," Stonewall cautioned. "It could be some renegade group who is responsible."

"Whoever did this is in possession of superior technology," Peters said. "We want to be careful tangling with them."

"This should not go unpunished," Mendez growled. "It won't go unpunished, I promise. We will not be intimidated by this brutal display of force."

"We should look for survivors," Demi pleaded. Houston could tell by her voice she was in shock but ready to deal with anything.

"I doubt we'll find any," Stonewall said, scanning the area with a pair of field glasses. "Anyone who survived the initial onslaught was taken care of by the large predators who would have been the first to arrive."

"We'll wait for a while in case somebody managed to get away and is hiding in the protection of the surrounding jungle." Stonewall decided.

"Unless they found a fortress there is little chance of surviving in this jungle." Houston didn't want to be the pessimistic one of the group, but he didn't have any hopes of finding anyone alive.

"You're right," Peters agreed, "but we can't dismiss it so easily. I agree with Stonewall. We wait."

"I still say we should go and check inside those habitats in case somebody lies there wounded and can't get out," Demi said.

"I'll go," Houston said. He looked at the other three men. "Two is better than one."

Stonewall cleared his throat. "All right, I'll come."

"I'd go with you," Mendez said to Houston's surprise, "but someone will have to man the cannon in case something big decides to investigate you two fools."

They stepped out of the tank onto the soft soil. A blast of hot, humid air greeted them and with it came the unpleasant odor of melted plasteel. Houston stared at the pile of white bones, realizing this had once been a living Human. The flesh had been stripped off clean, but the stench of death seemed to linger on.

He peered into the destroyed habitat. He saw pots and other utensils strewn across the floor. Some ripped-apart clothing and other shredded, now unidentifiable items covered one corner, but nothing else.

Houston had never seen this type of habitats before. They were small but large enough to sleep two people and leave some room for storage.

They walked on carefully, eyes roaming their surroundings as they walked. Houston held his flash rifle like a man who expected an enemy to appear at any moment, which was not far from the truth. Even though the large carnosaurs didn't seem to move as fast as their smaller cousins, their sheer size and long legs let them cross distances at terrific speed. They could not depend on the Trooper reacting fast enough to deal with such a sudden threat.

The pack of scavengers by the second habitat hissed loudly with open mouths, displaying strong teeth. Stonewall cursed and fired a shot into them, killing at least two and possibly wounding a couple more. The survivors screamed defiantly but retreated, pulling their two dead companions with them.

This time they found half of a skeleton inside the habitat. The other half lay outside, the bones torn apart. Of the long leg bones only splinters were left, evidence of large lizards having paid a visit. The skull was nowhere to be seen.

After an hour, they realized that there weren't any survivors, and they went back to the tank.

"Let's go," Stonewall said tonelessly.

The tank rumbled on toward Raptor's Tooth.

Everyone sat in silence. Nobody wanted to be the first one to talk. When they came to a swampy area, Mendez slowed down even more and maneuvered the tank carefully through the bog, ever so careful not to be swallowed up by quicksand from which even the tank might not be able to emerge.

He was the first one to break the silence. "I'm wondering if there is anything left of Raptor's Tooth, since nobody has heard from them after that cryptic message."

"Maybe the message didn't originate in Raptor's Tooth," Peters said.

"What message?" Tara's trembling voice showed her sudden fear.

"I would also be interested in that message?" Houston looked at Stonewall and Peters. "There is something you are not telling us?"

Stonewall threw a glance at the Trooper before he answered. "You are right. We've been holding back. The office of the Trading Commission received a message a few days ago from someone claiming that they were attacked by an aircraft. The message mentioned reptilians. That's all we know. We are on our way to investigate it. We were led to believe the message came from Raptor's Tooth."

"Why didn't you tell us that?" Tara asked. "What would have been the harm to know?"

"We didn't see any need for it." Peters made an apologetic gesture.

"I know. That idiotic military thing. Keep everything secret from the public until it is too late. There might be just some civilian out there who could make a helpful suggestion. The Military and the government can't allow that," Tara said bitterly.

"What would you have done with that knowledge?" Mendez challenged her.

"Nothing, but I might have been prepared for what we saw back there." A sob escaped her mouth. "My brother may be in Raptor's Tooth. I have come far and gone through much pain to find him. What irony should he be dead now that I'm so close."

Houston got up from his seat and put an arm around her shoulder. "Don't despair. There is still hope. Like Peters said, that message may not have come from Raptor's Tooth."

"I hope so." She wiped her eyes.

The tank climbed out of the swamp back on dry land, and Mendez increased the speed. After about thirty minutes or so they broke into another clearing, another mining camp. Houston saw a couple of habitats that had been partially destroyed. A few men in the camouflage outfits of the prospectors stood in a small clump between two habitats that seemed intact. They looked up when they became aware of the tank and reached for their flash rifles.

"Let me go first," Stonewall said. He opened the exit door and stepped out. When the men saw him in his Scouts uniform, they relaxed and waited for him to approach them.

"I believe it's safe to go out," Mendez said. Grabbing his rifle, he jumped onto the ground outside. Peters was the next one to leave the tank.

"Maybe you should stay inside," Houston said to the two women. They nodded.

"Call me if you need me," Demi said.

Houston joined the other men outside. Out of habit, he carried his flash rifle in both hands. He looked around and saw a couple of men lying on the ground not far away.

"What happened here?" he asked.

One of the prospectors looked at him but didn't say anything. Stonewall answered instead. "They were attacked by what appears to be Reptilians."

"They were vampires." The prospector pointed at one of the corpses. "Go, look for yourself."

Houston walked over to the man on the ground. His shirt had been ripped off his upper body. Houston noticed the unusual white complexion of the bare skin. He bent to look at the man's neck and discovered two puncture wounds.

One of the scouts, Peters, had followed him. He put a finger against the dead man's vein and nodded. "He's dead...and cold. Apparently, this happened only this morning. He shouldn't so cold. Not in this temperature."

"What do you think?" Houston asked.

"It appears the man has been drained of all his blood," Peters said. "But it doesn't seem that an animal, like the Bloodfrogs, did this. There are no other wounds on the body."

"Vampires! They were vampires," the prospector called with a loud voice. "And they were females."

"Did you see them?" Peters asked.

"Me and Sven came back from digging in our mine when we saw this teardrop-shaped craft land. Three figures jumped out and we knew immediately they were not human. They had green skin, bald heads with a stiff fin sticking up. And they were female. Couldn't miss their breasts. Besides, they didn't wear any clothes." He looked at one of the other men. "Right Sven?"

Sven nodded.

"So what happened after they landed?" Stonewall asked.

"Mark and Dmitri were the only ones in camp. They greeted the visitors, who acted friendly, as far as we could determine from our hiding place back there," Sven pointed into the jungle. "Then everything happened fast. There was nothing we could do. Before we realized it, both Mark and Dmitri were lying on the ground, two of the alien females straddled them and...it looked like they were having sex...at least that's what we thought. I mean...they went through the motions. You know...kissing and everything. When they got up, the third one took her turn on both men. When she was finally done, Mark and Dmitri lay on the ground. They didn't move." He shook his head. "We should have done something."

"We couldn't do a thing," the first prospector said. "Those females climbed back into their flier and bombed two of the habitats. They melted as if they were made of plastic. We hid until they were gone and when we checked on Mark, we saw he was dead. So was Dmitri. They didn't have a drop of blood left in their bodies." He stared at Mendez as if seeing him for the first time. "What's a Union Trooper doing here? Did a war break out or something?"

"Not yet but we may be at the brink of one," Mendez said.

"With the Dragons?"

"Not with the Dragons, but there is a Spider battleship sitting at the edge of this system," Stonewall said.

"Stonewall!" Mendez thundered. "May I remind you...?"

"Shut up, Trooper Mendez," Stonewall said with a tight voice. "These people have a right to know."

"I'm confused," Sven said. "These attackers were Reptilians, not Spiders."

"We are as confused as you are," Stonewall said. "We are here to find out what is going on."

Houston was as surprised as the prospector to hear about the Spider ship. He cursed the Trooper with all his secrets. Of course, the Scouts had known about it also. They were to blame as much as Mendez.

"Is there anything you men need before we leave?" Stonewall asked.

"No, nothing. We're good." Sven looked at the other prospectors. "We'll bury our friends and hope those females don't come back. Maybe we'll pull up stakes and setup camp somewhere else."

The others nodded in agreement. "Where are you heading anyway?" one of them asked.

"Raptor's Tooth. Heard anything from there?"

"No. Nothing. Not for a while anyway."

"All right. I guess we'll move on." Stonewall tipped his helmet.

Houston and Peters did the same. Mendez just grunted something and turned away. They climbed into the tank in silence.

Houston looked back at the camp before the tank disappeared in the jungle. The seven men were still standing in a group, probably deciding what to do next. He turned away and watched the sky above them. Suddenly, he didn't feel quiet as safe inside the tank. "How vulnerable are we in here, Trooper?" he asked.

"We should be safe," Mendez assured him. "The canopy of the tank is not made of the same material as those personal habitats. The Military uses superior technology."

"Well, I'm glad to hear that, but can we be sure?"

"I guess we'll find out," Mendez answered.

"When will that be?"

"Most likely right now," Mendez said. "Take over the reigns," he ordered Peters, while he rushed to the back of the tank and took his position in the seat that held the controls for the flash-cannon mounted in the rear.

Alarmed, Houston looked up and saw a tear-shaped object hovering above them. A blinding flash caused him to close his eyes involuntarily, and a loud crash made him realize they were under attack. He was momentarily blinded from the flash and expected the invisible dome above him to melt. Without thinking he threw his body across the isle to cover Tara.

The tank rocked dangerously but the canopy seemed to hold. He opened his eyes, still seeing white flecks of light in front of him. "Are you okay?" he asked.

"If you get off me so I can breathe I will be," Tara moaned.

"Stay in your seats," Mendez shouted. "That's the safest place." He seemed to fiddle with the controls of the cannon.

Houston turned to look at him in time to see him push the firing stud. Lifting his eyes, he saw the white flash hit the alien vessel. It was enveloped by a fiery glow for an eternal moment before it exploded. Melted shards of metal rained from the sky and disappeared in the underbrush of the jungle.

After Houston recovered his full sight, he searched the sky and ground, but there was nothing left of the alien vessel to even suggest it ever existed.

"I believe we just proved that those invaders are no match for our firepower," Mendez said with a triumphant grin.

"Don't feel so smug too soon," Stonewall warned. "That feeling of superiority can be dangerous."

"As you've noticed they can't touch us with their weapon, but ours destroyed them. What additional proof do you need, Master Scout?"

"None, I hope. I still think we should not rush into anything."

"They attacked us first, Stonewall. And did you forget the dead men in those camps back there already?"

"No, but I'll advise caution anyway."

"Scouts!" Mendez spat, obviously disgusted. "Always advising caution when action is required. I guess that's why I'm a Trooper and you are what you are."

Stonewall didn't reply and neither did Scout Peters. Houston had to agree with Mendez. Action had been required and he had acted swiftly and with positive results. There was no telling if a second hit from the alien vessel would have left them unscathed. He was not a military man, but he knew enough of weaponry to know that the artificial intelligence that was used to control the more destructive weapons learned and adjusted to conditions. They didn't know anything about their attackers and taking the cautious approach could have been fatal.

"Congratulations, Trooper Mendez," he said. "You may have saved our lives."

Mendez threw him an amused look. "I *did* save your lives. I hope you remember that."

"I have to agree with you, Mendez," Demi said, "you acted properly, and we have to thank you for saving our skin. I hope that was the only craft. I don't know if I can stay so calm the next time."

"Don't worry. Should there be another one, I'll deal with it the same way I dealt with this one." Mendez surveyed the area around and above them. "I think I'll stay back here, just in case. Next time I won't wait this long. I'll blast them out of the sky the moment I see them."

"That's what I'm afraid of," Stonewall murmured.

Houston wished he had the Trooper's confidence.

With Peters at the controls, the tank rumbled on through thick vines and fields of mushrooms. The scenery outside had not changed much; the same giant mushrooms and sometimes large groups of the conifer-like trees.

They drove along a large lake for a while and then the trail led back into the jungle.

"How long is it still to Raptor's Tooth?" Tara asked.

Peters looked at the gauges. "According to this we should be there any time now." He halted the tank with a little curse. "In fact, I believe we have arrived."

"So do I," Stonewall said.

Houston didn't see it at first, but when four men carrying flash rifles, aimed at the tank, appeared in front of them, he realized that they had arrived in a place where Humans lived. Then he saw the crack in the thick trunk of one of the mushroom trees and recognized it for what if was...the entrance to a hiding place inside the tree. A relatively safe place on Epsilon. He had used places like that himself when he traveled in the jungle.

Peters was the first one to leave the tank. He left his rifle behind and had his hands up in the air as he walked toward the four men. After a few moments of talking with the men, they lowered their rifles. One of them came toward the tank and looked inside.

"Welcome to Raptor's Tooth," he said. Spying Tara and Demi, he smiled. "Two beautiful women. I hope you're single."

"Hi," Demi said. "I'm a nurse and I am single."

"And I am Tara." She smiled. "I'm single also, but..." she shrugged and looked at Houston. "Hopefully for not much longer."

"Welcome anyway. I'm Alexandrov." The man's expression changed and became serious. "You haven't picked a good time for a visit."

"Why not?" Houston asked.

"We've had some trouble. There's going to be a meeting. You're welcome to attend." He stared at Mendez. "Hello there, Trooper.

There must be a reason you are here. I hope it has something to do with our problem."

"It depends what problem you are talking about," Mendez said.

"You'll find out. Come with us to the meeting." The man moved away so they could leave the tank. Houston slapped on his helmet, took his flash rifle, and slung it across his shoulder. He hoped he wouldn't need it.

"Ever been to Raptor's Tooth?" the prospector asked Houston who walked beside him.

"No, can't say I had the pleasure." Houston smiled. Then he held out his hand. "I'm Dave."

"Well, pleased to meet you, Dave. You can call me Frisky. Don't ask me why. It's a long story." The other man grinned. "That little redhead is with you?"

Houston nodded. "Yes."

"Girls like her don't belong here, you know. Hold on to her."

"She's tougher than she looks."

"That's the problem...her looks. Most of the women here aren't that beautiful, and there aren't many around. She could spell trouble."

"That's where I come in...I'm her protector."

They came out in an area that had been cleared of some of the tall mushroom trees and most of the low-growing vegetation. A few of the small habitats Houston had seen in the other two camps were situated in a circle in the center. Houston saw that at least three of them were damaged.

He didn't really have to ask how they came to be damaged, but he asked it anyway, "What happened to those habitats?"

"We had visitors. Unfriendly visitors."

"Female Reptilians?"

Frisky stopped walking and looked at him. "How did you know they were Reptilians?"

"We ran into them on the way. They destroyed one mining camp, killed everyone there, did some damage in the last camp, and killed a couple of prospectors in that one. We shot down one of their fliers after they attacked us."

"That's a bit of good news. That means they're not invincible. They weren't all females, by the way. Some of them were males."

"Supposedly they are vampires."

"They probably are...among other things." They started walking again to catch up with the others.

"Did you have any casualties?" Houston didn't see any bodies on the ground, which of course didn't mean anything.

"They killed Ludwig, sucked him dry. One of the females raped Vincini while one of the males sucked the blood from his veins. We shot and wounded him but couldn't save Vincini. Silverstone was lucky. We got here in time to chase off the female who rode him like a bitch gone crazy. He doesn't remember a thing. Poor guy got his arm chewed up badly by another of the males."

"What do you mean?" Houston asked, perplexed. "Are you saying they were trying to eat him?"

"That's what it looked like."

"How many ships were there?"

"Two."

They had caught up with the others. Tara came and leaned on Houston. "Everything all right?" she asked with a low voice.

"Everything's fine," Houston said. "Under the circumstances."

"Did you say you were a nurse?" Frisky asked her.

She shook her head. "No but Demi is. Why?"

"Perhaps she can stitch up Silverstone's arm. We don't have anyone here who is actually qualified to do that kind of stuff."

"You'll have to talk to her."

"I'll let Hershey do that." He poked one of the other three prospectors in the arm. "Listen, Hersh, take this lady to Silverstone and have her look at his arm. She's a nurse." He looked at Demi. "You are that kind of a nurse, aren't you?"

She nodded. "I hope you have some medicines and equipment I can use."

"Whatever we have will have to do. Hershey will show you everything."

"Let's hurry then," the man named Hershey said. "Silverstone is barely hanging on. He needs medical attention badly."

Demi gave Stonewall a questioning look. The Scout nodded, "Go ahead." Then he looked at Houston. "Are you and your lady friend still planning to stay in Raptor's Tooth?" he asked. "Or have you seen enough."

"We've seen more than enough, but we still have to find Tara's brother."

"Well, if there is nothing more to see here for you, we might as well head for the meeting hall," Alexandrov said.

"Is this all there is of Raptor's Tooth?" Houston asked Frisky.

Alexandrov laughed. "No. You'll find that Raptor's Tooth is unlike any other community you've seen on Epsilon," he said, smiling cryptically.

They left the cleared area and walked back into the jungle.

"Where does everyone live?" Tara asked.

"Inside the trees," Frisky said. "And up in the trees. Look up."

Houston looked up toward the top of the mushrooms. At first, he didn't know what he was supposed to see, but then he spied the bulges on the stems of a few of them. Somehow, they didn't look like parts of the stem. The huge tree in front of them had some kind of structure attached to the bottom of the umbrella.

"These are abandoned Queel-hives."

"Queel-hives?" Tara asked. "I don't know what they are."

"The Queel are the equivalent of bees on Epsilon, only these are huge, like the ants here, and intelligent. They build their hives around the mushroom stems and under the umbrellas. We were lucky to discover these. Can't get any safer places to live in."

"I understand. Like Epsilon City except you live in the trees." Tara said. "Ingenious."

"We Humans are a remarkable race," Frisky said. "We are not strong, not fast. We can't fly or breathe under water. We can't jump high or do many other things necessary for survival, but we have one thing...a brain, and we can adapt. That's why we survive even on a hostile planet like Epsilon."

"How do we get up there?" Stonewall asked.

Frisky pointed at an opening in the massive mushroom stem. "That way, please." He led the group into a room inside the mushroom. A basket-like contraption with a flat bottom and a railing sat on the floor, supported by thick cables that hung down from a hole in the ceiling.

"Our elevator. Don't be afraid to step into it. It is quite safe." He looked the group over and added, "We'll have to split up. Eight people is a bit too much I'm afraid."

"We'll take the next turn," Stonewall said. He looked at Mendez. "You accompany Mr. Houston and the young lady. Peters and I will join these other two gentlemen later."

The Trooper nodded. "No problem." He was the first one to step onto the platform.

Houston looked at Tara. "Go ahead. I'll be right behind you."

Frisky pulled on the ropes and the elevator began moving upward into the shaft above them. "Muscle power," he explained. "We have an ingenious system that uses a second elevator as counterweight. One goes up, the other one comes down. That way there is always an elevator available."

It didn't take long until they arrived at the top. They met the other elevator halfway up. It was empty.

Stepping out of the elevator and onto a solid floor created the illusion that they were still on the ground, but Houston knew that below the hard floor was a whole lot of nothing...nothing but air.

Tara looked around her with large eyes. "This is a hive? A beehive?"

The prospector chuckled. "We've done some renovations but, yes, this is an actual beehive. A marvel of engineering, isn't it?"

"Wonderful. It is hard to believe we are at the top of a mushroom tree. And it's so pleasantly cool in here. How many people live up here?"

"A couple hundred or so, but many are not here. Some of the prospectors are out working their claims or looking for gems." He shrugged. "Some may never come back. This is Epsilon."

They waited for the other men to come up. Once the two Scouts and the other two prospectors joined them, they walked further into the corridor that stretched ahead of them. The corridor was lit up by minisuns, and Houston could see openings leading into what looked like small rooms.

"These are storage rooms," Frisky explained. "Most of us live on the upper floors."

They climbed a set of stairs and stepped into an oval room. Houston saw two corridors; they followed one for a short distance until they came to a second staircase. "Up this way," Frisky said.

At the top of those stairs was a larger room. A number of corridors led away from it. They walked down one of them.

"The meeting won't be until four o'clock. Perhaps you'd be interested and having something to eat?" Frisky gave them a hopeful look. "I haven't eaten anything since this morning. We have only one place here...*The Big Rex*. The food is good."

"I wouldn't mind having something to eat," Stonewall said.

"I'm kind of hungry too." Tara looked at Houston. "How about you?"

"Sure. We have nothing else to do anyway."

The Big Rex was a nice, cozy looking place. The waitress, a homely looking young woman, gave the Trooper an inquiring look. Turning her attention to Stonewall, she smiled, "I've always had a thing for men in uniforms," she said. "But I have a feeling you're not here for pleasure."

"I'm afraid not," the big Scout told her.

"Hi, Martina," Frisky said. "Do you have a table for us?"

"You're lucky." She scanned the room. "We've been quite busy this morning and at lunchtime, but now it has slowed down a bit. Are you going to the meeting?"

"We are planning to." Frisky squinted at her. "Why such a gloomy expression?"

"I have nothing to smile about. Everyone seems to be scared right now."

"Well, they have a right to be scared." He glanced at the Trooper. "But maybe things will take a turn for the better, now that the Military has arrived."

She led them to a couple of tables and took their orders. Houston found he was quite hungry, despite the horrible things they all had witnessed. He hoped the prospector's hopes were warranted. What they had seen left plenty of room for speculation. He was curious what they would find out at the meeting.

After they finished eating, Frisky led them down another corridor. It ended in a room as large as a meeting hall. Benches made from tree branches and roots were set up in rows and Houston realized that it was actually a meeting hall. Many of the benches were already occupied by a number of people.

"Take a seat, please," Frisky said.

They chose a row of empty benches in the back and sat down. A short, squat man, who stood in the front, looked at the group. He waved and Frisky waved back.

"I see we have some newcomers here today," the man said loudly so everyone could here him. "Even a Union Trooper and a couple of Scouts by the looks of it. Welcome to Raptor's Tooth." He looked over the assembled crowd. "As most of you know by now, we've been attacked by an unknown vessel. The people who attacked us were Reptilians. Apparently. It was an act of aggression not toward us but toward all Humans on this planet. In a moment we may all find out why that happened and what we are facing." He lifted his hand to acknowledge a man coming in through another entrance. Then his gaze came back to Houston's group.

"Perhaps the arrival of the Trooper means that the rest of Epsilon has experienced similar attacks. We will ask him later, but first I'd like you to listen to someone who just came back from a bizarre and frightening journey. He has a remarkable tale to tell. His unusual return to Raptor's Tooth and the attack on our camp leave no doubt that he is speaking the truth. I urge you all to listen to what he has to tell us. Please, welcome my good friend Gilbert Turner."

————

Read the conclusion of
The Stonewall Chronicles
in Book Three
MYSTERIES OF EPSILON
Available Soon from Melange Books

————

Don't miss out on your next favorite book!

Join the Melange Books mailing list at
www.melange-books.com/mail.html

ABOUT THE AUTHOR

Herbert lives near Winnipeg, Canada. He spends his free time spinning tales about imaginary worlds and the strange creatures inhabiting them. His first published story `The Anniversary Gift' appeared in `Sweet Revenge' published by Midnight Showcase. Even though he writes in other genres, his love is Science Fiction. He enjoys building alien worlds and societies. Most of his stories contain an element of Erotica. All of his books are available from Melange Books.

Website: www.fictitioustales.weebly.com
Blog: hegro.blogspot.com
Blog: hergros.blogspot.com
Email: hegro@shaw.ca

ALSO BY HERBERT GROSSHANS

NOVELS
Bullet of Revenge

A Matter of Justice

Mark of the Cobra

Orola

Orion

RHODAR SERIES
Clouds Over Maridaan

OPERATION STARGATE SERIES
Codename Salamander

Savanna

The Aregon Files, Vol. 1

The Aregone Files, Vol.2 (available early 2024)

SEEDS OF CHAOS DUOLOGY
Eden's Gate

Hell's Gate

STARDOGS DUOLOGY
Return to Redsky

Redemption

STARS IN CHAINS DUOLOGY
Slave

Liberator

WEB OF CONSPIRACY TRILOGY

Death of a Hero

Traitors and Patriots

Tarnished Valor

THE XANDRA SERIES

Daughter of the Dark

Mother of Light

Goddess of Life

Lure of Seduction

Escape from Paradise

Iceworld

Alien World

Dark World

SHORT STORY COLLECTIONS

Dual Visions

Tapestry of Dreams

Time Flares